"I have no intent[ion] with you, Jan."

"But, Nick, I want a real marriage," Jan retorted. "Not some farce where we live in the same house and sleep in different beds."

Abruptly she changed tactics, discarding her antagonism…along with her robe. Lifting her bare arms to his chest, she gazed seductively into his smoldering eyes.

"Give in, Nick," she urged huskily. "If you don't make love to me tonight I'll just keep after you until you do. I'll walk around the house without a stitch on, and I'll sneak into your bed. I'll kiss you until you can't hold back anymore and you *have* to take me."

"Heaven help me," he groaned, and she knew she had won….

THE AUTHOR

Lynn Turner's love for living is obvious in the strongly emotional stories she writes. She's a warm and enthusiastic person who gets in the mood for writing by listening to Sousa march music.

A full-time writer, Lynn also keeps house for her husband and two sons. However, she has a button that says The Only Thing Domestic About Me Is That I Was Born In This Country. One of her favorite pastimes is staying up late watching horror movies on TV.

Books by Lynn Turner

HARLEQUIN TEMPTATION
 8—FOR NOW, FOR ALWAYS
56—ANOTHER DAWN

HARLEQUIN SUPERROMANCE
 65—A PERSISTENT FLAME
134—A LASTING GIFT

These books may be available at your local bookseller.

Don't miss any of our special offers. Write to us at the following address for information on our newest releases.

Harlequin Reader Service
P.O. Box 52040, Phoenix, AZ 85072-2040
Canadian address: P.O. Box 2800, Postal Station A,
5170 Yonge St., Willowdale, Ont. M2N 6J3

Another Dawn

LYNN TURNER

Harlequin Books

TORONTO • NEW YORK • LONDON
AMSTERDAM • PARIS • SYDNEY • HAMBURG
STOCKHOLM • ATHENS • TOKYO • MILAN

Published April 1985

ISBN 0-373-25156-4

Printed in Canada

1

JANET ST. CLAIR heard the plane long before she saw
it, while it was no more than a droning buzz like
that of a large winged insect. She remained squatting
on the hard-packed earth, the camera fitted with its
bulky macrozoom lens held firmly but absently as
she cocked her head to listen. The four-and-a-half-
foot diamondback rattler she'd been preparing to
shoot slithered away unnoticed as she slowly rose to
her feet, facing slightly northeast, her eyes narrowed
against the glare of the late-morning sun. She was
totally still, and there was an attitude of poised ex-
pectancy about her.

She was tall, almost five foot ten, reed slim and
long-legged, and the heritage of her mother's Hopi
Indian forebears was recognizable in the burnished
copper of her skin and the sleek curtain of inky hair
down her back. The only evidence of her paternal
ancestry lay in the vivid blue of her eyes, startling
against her dusky complexion.

For almost a full minute she stood, silent and motionless, and then the plane appeared as a speck
against the cloudless New Mexico sky. Within seconds she had identified it, even at that distance, and
a wide smile bared perfect white teeth and warmed
her classic features. At that moment, she became
breathtakingly beautiful.

"Nick!"

The name was an elated whisper as she suddenly

exploded into action, flying down a rocky slope to the place where a buckskin horse was tethered. On the way she unslung the camera from her neck and was already stowing it in the specially designed case hanging from the saddle as her right foot searched for the offside stirrup.

"He's back, Sandy," she said to the big gelding as she gathered the reins in one hand. Her heels nudged his flanks. "Come on, boy, let's see if we can beat him home."

It was a good five-mile ride back to the house, four miles farther than the landing strip on which the twin-engine Cessna would set down. The woman leaned low over the horse's neck as his long legs ate up the distance, his hooves kicking up puffs of dust that became a rolling cloud in their wake as she headed him toward the low, rambling whitewashed adobe house and the man who would be waiting there—if she didn't arrive first.

Above the drumming of the buckskin's hooves on the compacted earth another sound reached her, and she glanced back over her shoulder, her hair flapping around her face like a raven's wings. Her laugh was snatched away by the wind as she faced forward again, sighting between the gelding's ears as she judged the distance they still had to cover. They just might make it, she decided, and the heels of her boots urged an extra measure of speed from the big horse.

The plane had made a wide sweep to the west before heading in toward the bare dirt landing strip, and the pilot had spotted her. She darted another quick look rearward. He had banked sharply, but was now leveling out to come in from behind her, low and fast. At the last moment the plane's nose lifted, and the right wingtip dipped toward the

earth. Jan felt the shock wave of the Cessna's passing, and had a brief glimpse of flashing teeth in a
face almost as brown as her own through the cock-
pit window before the pilot climbed away to the
right, to an altitude great enough to permit the safe
execution of his next maneuver. The gleaming
blue-and-white craft seemed to stand on one wing
as it completed a perfect 360-degree turn and then
zoomed back over her head, the wings waggling in
farewell.

"Grandstanding show-off," Jan muttered with a
grin, then flicked the ends of the reins against the
buckskin's side.

She rode straight onto the paved patio behind the
house, vaulting from the saddle before the horse had
come to a full stop. Her boots skidding on the glazed
tiles, she caught wildly at the frame with one hand
and shoved the heavy double-glazed sliding door
along its track with the other. She burst into the
house from the back at precisely the same moment
that Nick Alexander threw the door open and
lunged inside from the front.

They faced each other across an open, sunny living room and a spacious entry hall, both panting
after the final sprint to get inside first. Nick broke
into a grin as he dropped his black cowhide suitcase
and sagged against a stuccoed wall.

"You crazy little savage, you'll break your fool
neck on that horse one of these days."

"If you don't kill me first playing dive-bomber,"
Jan retorted. "You darn near took my head off!"

He laughed as he reached up to remove the avia-
tor sunglasses concealing his sea-green eyes behind
silver lenses.

"Hell, I had at least two feet of clearance." Then
he smiled crookedly. "Miss me?"

"What's to miss?" Jan quipped. But she was smiling, too.

He shoved away from the wall, and they met in the center of the room. Nick lifted her off the floor in a huge bear hug, then planted a noisy, deliberately wet kiss on her cheek.

"I missed *you*, and that's a fact," he said as he set her on her feet again. Jan grimaced and wiped at her cheek, and he chuckled.

"I need a hot shower and a change of clothes. Any beer in the house?"

"I've had a six-pack waiting in the fridge since Tuesday," Jan said, and he dropped a light, appreciative kiss on her forehead.

"I knew there was a reason I keep you around."

Jan rolled her eyes with a long-suffering sigh. Nick grinned again, gave her bottom an affectionate swat, then headed for his room. As he reached the hall he turned back with a frown, stabbing a finger in her direction.

"And get that beast off my patio before he leaves another souvenir for me to step in on the way to the pool!"

While he was showering and changing Jan returned Sandy to the lean-to that served as his stable, giving him an extra portion of feed after she'd finished rubbing him down. Then she dropped her photographic equipment off at the three-room bungalow behind the main house. While she was there, she washed her face and hands and ran a brush through her hair to clean the dust out of it. *No use bothering with makeup,* she thought ruefully as she gazed at her reflection in the mirror; *he wouldn't notice, anyway.*

It was the great despair of her life that while she loved Nick Alexander with a burning, soul-consuming, sometimes agonizing intensity, he always had and always would look upon her as an alternately exasperating and amusing child — a playmate, almost.

She had fallen in love with him fifteen years ago, when she was ten and he was twenty. Her father had been city editor of the large Eastern newspaper Nick had just come to work for as an investigative reporter. Evan St. Clair had perceived the younger man's potential at once. Nick quickly became his protégé and, eventually, the paper's star reporter.

The first time Evan brought him home to dinner, Jan had been literally struck dumb. Never in her young life had she seen such a beautiful man: tall and athletically muscular, with colossal (to her, at that time) shoulders and a trim waist and hips. His hair was thick and dark and seemed to possess a will all its own; even now it was in a constant state of disarray. His face was that of a movie star — a young Cary Grant, perhaps — and he had the most gorgeous green eyes, clear and keenly intelligent, but with a wicked, almost fiendish humor lurking in their shadowed depths.

And she, in her pigtails and the hideous retainer that rotten, child-hating orthodontist had convinced her parents she had to wear, could only stand and gape like a retarded fool when her father led him over and introduced them.

Nick, of course, had known. He had been kind and sweet, never patronizing or talking down to her, making her his slave for the next thousand years by pretending not to notice the adoring, worshipful looks she kept sliding at him. He even drew her into the conversation from time to time, as if he really believed a ten-year-old might have something worthwhile to contribute.

Over the years her awed hero worship had developed into something much deeper and stronger. Seeing the change in her—she no longer stammered like a ninny in his presence and had learned to disguise her passionate devotion as mere fondness—he had assumed she was over her case of puppy love and allowed a real friendship to develop between them. He talked to her, really *talked* to her, about the things that were important to him.

He swore her to secrecy, then confided that it was his most cherished dream to someday write books: novels that would stir people, move them, take them outside themselves and into other worlds, other places, other lives. Jan listened in solemn silence, and then told him that he was making a mistake to think of it as a dream; that if that was what he really wanted to do, he should stop thinking in terms of "someday" and begin *now*. Nick looked at her for a full minute with the strangest expression, as if he hadn't heard her or thought he'd misunderstood what she'd said, and then his face split in a blinding, ear-to-ear grin and he told her that, by God, she was right!

His first novel sold the week before he was hired by UPI and sent to Vietnam as a correspondent. For three years he shuttled back and forth across the globe, reporting the war and its aftermath in stories that earned him a foot locker full of awards. During those three years Jan worried incessantly. What if he caught malaria or typhoid? What if a sniper mistook him for a soldier, or what if his jeep hit a mine, or he fell into one of those tiger pits she'd read about, or— There were a million and one "what ifs," and it seemed all of them occurred to her at one time or another.

When he finally returned for good she knew a brief time of peace, but it was not to last. His book had been an enormous success, holding a place on the best-seller lists for almost six months, and almost as soon as Nick set foot on American soil again he was whisked off for a publicity tour and then on to Los Angeles to collaborate on the screenplay based on his novel. While there, he met an up-and-coming young starlet named Marina Calhoun. Jan learned of their marriage the same way as everybody else had—she read about it in the morning paper.

Her world seemed to crumble around her. Nick— *her* Nick—married to someone else! Shock gave way to depression and despair, and she moped around the house for days. Didn't he know, couldn't he sense with that incredible insight that she'd been waiting, hoping, planning for the day when she would be old enough and sophisticated enough to take her place at his side? Apparently not, she decided with a dismal feeling of rejection. Or else he did know and just didn't care. But that possibility was too terrible even to contemplate, and so she didn't.

The marriage did not run smoothly, even from the beginning. Marina was a spoiled, willful flirt, used to having her own way and being the center of attention. She did not take kindly to the publicity given Nick's book, the successful movie based on it—in which she hadn't been able to win even a minor part—or Nick himself. The situation worsened when a second book was published to even greater acclaim than the first, and then a third. Marital discord seemed to have a beneficial effect on Nick's creativity, at least. The more turbulent his marriage became, the more inspired was his writing. Finally, after several separations and stormy attempts at reconciliation, Marina filed for divorce. Jan was overjoyed, and hopeful. The marriage had lasted four years, and during that time she had grown into a nineteen-year-old woman of stunning looks and mature self-possession.

But did Nick notice? Did he suddenly see her with new eyes and smack his head with his palm and exclaim, "Wow! To think I've wasted four years with that Hollywood floozy when I could have had *you!*"

He did not. He continued to make sporadic visits to her parents' home, usually while she was away at college, and once in a rare while he condescended to visit her on campus. Jan remembered one such visit in particular. As they walked across the quad, he started teasing her about the men in her life. A red fog suddenly obscured her vision, and she almost hit him over the head with the stack of textbooks she was lugging, which he typically had not offered to carry for her.

That was the day she finally accepted that he would never love her the way she loved him, and decided to content herself with whatever feeling he did have for her. She switched majors in the middle of her sophomore year, going for a degree in journalism. Her father, in his ignorance, was thrilled. He believed the decision had been motivated by a desire to emulate him. In fact, Jan had concluded that if she couldn't be Nick's lover she would at least earn his respect by succeeding in his field. And she did. She virtually took over the student newspaper, published articles in several literary journals, and even sold a couple of short stories to *The New Yorker*. Even more gratifying than the praise and various accolades she received, though, was Nick's offhand compliment when he phoned after reading one of the short stories.

"Not half-bad, kid. We might make a writer out of you yet."

Her feet hardly touched the ground for days.

When she graduated summa cum laude, he was there, sitting beside her parents in the section reserved for family. Knowing his eyes were on her, Jan had all she could do to keep from tripping over her own feet, and when he gave her a brotherly kiss of congratulation she was afraid she might faint from sheer ecstasy. He intensified her euphoria by drawing her off to one side, guiding her with a hand placed casually at her waist to stand beneath an enormous spreading maple tree.

"Decided what you're gonna do with all that fancy book-learnin'?" he asked with a grin.

Jan shook her head, employment the furthest thing from her mind at that moment. "Not yet. I've had a couple of offers from syndicates, and one from one of the slick women's magazines, but—"

"That's not for you." Nick vetoed the last suggestion firmly. "You'd suffocate. And you can always get a job as a reporter. Evan would hire you, even if nobody else would." Then he totally astounded her by asking, "How would you like to come to work for me for a while?"

Jan gaped at him stupidly before she found her tongue. "For you? Doing what?"

"Research assistant. At least that's what you can put on your W-2 form. I *hate* doing research. As far as I'm concerned, it's the least tolerable part of this whole writing business. Unfortunately, it's also a necessary part. I've read your stuff. You put a lot of work into researching your pieces. Do you enjoy it?"

Jan was dumbfounded, agog. He'd read her work? Not just that one story, but all of it? *Be still, my throbbing heart,* she thought giddily.

"Yes," she answered honestly. "I do enjoy re-

search...a lot. Digging into resource books, old
newspapers and microfilm records, learning things I
didn't know before—it's exciting.''

Nick nodded solemnly. ''I figured as much. It
shows in your writing. Your pieces never come out
dull or trite. You make any subject you tackle come
alive.''

Jan mumbled a dazed, ''Thank you.'' By now
she'd half convinced herself that she was dreaming
this entire conversation.

''So...it would seem we're a perfect match. What
do you say? Care to give it a try?''

She somehow mastered the urge to fling herself on
him and tell him that she'd scrub his floors and
shine his shoes for the rest of her life just to be near
him. What he was proposing was strictly a business
arrangement, and she was justifiably proud of herself as she replied that sure, it might be fun to work
with him, at least until something more interesting
came along.

That had been three years ago, and in those three
years Jan had assisted him in the completion of an
equal number of books. After a brief visit home,
she'd packed up her belongings and moved here, to
the isolated property Nick had just purchased in the
northern part of New Mexico. He'd had it with the
shallowness and hypocrisy on the West Coast, he'd
said, and neither did he relish the idea of returning
to the snobbish Eastern literary establishment. And
besides, weren't all best-selling authors supposed to
be eccentric recluses?

They had settled into an easy, comfortable relationship during the past three years. If Nick didn't
exactly lust after her body, or feel a jolt like an elec-
tric shock when their eyes met, he *had* come to care
for her in a different way, she knew. A genuine af-

fection existed between them: not a flame, true, but a definite warmth when they were together. When he said he'd missed her during his trip to New York, Jan didn't doubt his sincerity. And that, she told herself as she turned for the front door of the bungalow, was more than enough to keep her with him—for the rest of her life, God willing.

She found him sprawled on the cream leather sofa in the living room, his bare feet sticking out of faded jeans and his checked shirt open to expose a hard, tanned chest covered with an abundance of wiry hair. There was more than a sprinkling of gray in that hair, Jan noticed, not for the first time. There were also faint wings of it at his temples. But Nick Alexander at thirty-five would have put a lot of twenty-year-old jocks to shame. As lean and fit as ever, his arms and legs well muscled and his stomach still a hard slab, Jan thought he'd probably change as little in the next fifteen years as he had in the past fifteen. When he heard the patio door slide shut he rolled his head on the back of the sofa to send her a smile as he held out an empty beer can.

"I need a refill. What took you so long?"

"I had to rub Sandy down and feed him, then get my camera and film out of the sun," Jan answered as she took the empty to the kitchen. She brought him another cold beer and handed it to him over the back of the sofa.

"What have you been capturing for posterity this time? Feeding vultures, or the bleached bones of some poor coyote?" Nick claimed that some of her pictures were downright gruesome in their attempts to accurately depict the various life cycles in the Great American West.

"Rattlesnakes, mainly," Jan said.

Nick grimaced as he pulled the tab on the can of

beer. "Yech! You have definitely got a perverted streak." He turned to look at her, then patted the sofa beside him. "Come over here and sit down."

Jan had been hoping for such an invitation. She went gladly, sinking down beside him, close, but not too close. Nick swigged from the fresh beer, then set it on an end table beside the sofa. Jan didn't scold him for his carelessness. She had personally applied several coats of polyurethane to every wooden surface in the room as soon as she realized how indifferent he was about where he deposited cans, bottles, glasses and ashtrays.

When he suddenly dipped his head to brush a soft kiss across her temple, she was more than just surprised. He was not normally given to such tender displays. The bone-cracking hug he'd subjected her to when he arrived was more his style: enthusiastic, vigorous and totally lacking in any recognition that hers was supposed to be the weaker sex. Jan looked at him sharply, and for the first time noticed the faint lines of weariness at eyes and mouth.

"You look tired. Have a rough week?" she asked softly. He had gone to New York to meet with his agent and the publisher who'd bought his latest manuscript.

"The pits."

His voice was uncharacteristically grim. Jan longed to reach up and smooth the creases from his face, pull his head down to her breast and cradle it there, but she curbed such foolish impulses before they could get out of hand.

"I saw Marina," he said abruptly, as his head fell back and he closed his eyes. Jan didn't respond, as a sudden fear clutched at her throat. "She was there with Leslie," he added, "ransacking every store on Fifth Avenue."

Leslie was Marina's daughter, the result of a brief teenage marriage. The girl had been farmed out to various relatives and boarding schools almost from infancy because her mother didn't think it would do her glamorous image any good to have a runny-nosed kid trailing along in her wake.

Careful to keep her voice casual, Jan asked, "How did you happen to meet them?"

Nick's mouth twisted cynically, but he didn't open his eyes. "It was a case of rotten luck. We just happened to be staying at the same hotel. We ran into one another in the lobby, and from then on they hounded me morning, noon and night." He hesitated, then added heavily, "She's making noises about a reconciliation. Wants to bring Leslie out for a visit."

Jan felt the blood pound in her ears, and the skin at the back of her neck prickled in apprehension. "Did you say they could come?"

"What do you think?" The response was dry as dust. "Not that knowing she isn't welcome will keep Marina from coming. That's got to be the most totally self-involved woman I've ever known!"

His eyes suddenly opened and he sat up, then half turned to slide an arm across Jan's shoulders and pull her against him.

"Thank goodness I've got you to protect me," he murmured, and she had the crazy, irrational impression that he wasn't joking. He lifted her chin with one bent finger and looked into her eyes. "You would, wouldn't you? If she came after me again, you'd be in my corner."

Emotion made Jan's voice a little husky as she replied. "That's a damned fool question, Alexander, and insulting on top of it. Whose corner do you *think* I'd be in?"

He smiled down at her, his beautifully sculpted mouth curving with a lazy sensuality that took her breath away. What she wouldn't give to have that mouth come down on hers in a hard, no-holds-barred kiss!

"That's my girl," Nick said softly, and then without warning both his arms went around her and he pressed her tight against his chest. "Hug me back." As usual, he didn't make it a request, but an order.

Jan slid her arms around his waist and squeezed, trying not to be too aware of the roughness of his chest hair against her cheek or the clean warmth of his skin, or the slow, regular thump and thud of his heart under her ear. Something was wrong here. She wasn't sure exactly what, but something was definitely amiss. She had the feeling that he *needed* to feel her arms around him, that he was drawing both comfort and strength from her. When he released her, she sat back to give him a level, direct look.

"All right," she said, "what's going on, here? All this—this business about Marina—was just leading up to something else, wasn't it? You've never needed protection from a woman in your life. It's usually the other way around," she added dryly. "So just spit it out, Nick. What is it you've been sneaking up to sideways?"

He pulled a wry face. "So much for tact and diplomacy," he muttered. Then he sighed as he swiveled to face her fully, one long leg bent at the knee and pulled onto the sofa between them. All trace of humor was suddenly gone from his eyes, and his mouth was compressed slightly, as if in distaste.

"I've been trying to think of a way to spring it on you all the way home," he said quietly. "But the simple fact is, there just isn't any good way."

He reached out to take her hands in his, and Jan's

fear returned in a sharp, alarming flash of premonition. Nick took a deep breath, seeming to brace himself, to gather resolve for whatever it was he had to say.

"First... you know that I love you."

It was a statement, not a question. Jan's initial reaction was stunned shock. Fortunately it was fleeting. Yes, she did know that he loved her, in a way. The fact that it wasn't the way she wanted made her soft smile a little bittersweet, a little pained, so that to Nick it might conceivably have looked apologetic or even tinged with sympathy.

"Yes," she murmured as she gave his hands a gentle squeeze. "I know. I love you, too."

The years of playing a part made it possible to say the words easily and naturally. She might have been speaking to her father, or any good friend; there was just that amount of warmth in her voice—just so much, and no more.

Something flickered briefly in Nick's eyes. She might have taken it for disappointment if that had made any sense. Then he returned the pressure of her fingers with a fleeting smile.

"You also know that I wouldn't hurt you for the world, don't you? If I could possibly help it?"

"Yes. I know that, too." Panic began to tug at Jan's stomach. Whatever he was leading up to, it must be pretty awful. She gazed at him silently, waiting, trying to brace herself for a blow when she had no idea with how much force or from what direction it would come.

He drew another long breath, his dark brows pulling together. "It's hard to know where to begin," he murmured. "You remember that little fender-bender I had a few months back?"

Jan nodded mutely. To call it a fender-bender was

a masterpiece of understatement. He had swerved suddenly to avoid hitting a large mongrel dog that belonged to their nearest neighbor, while traveling at a speed that was excessive even for him. The dog got away clean, without a scratch. Nick's Mercedes had rolled twice and was hardly recognizable as an automobile when it came to rest. Miraculously, he'd escaped with nothing more than some bruised ribs and a stiff neck.

"Well," he said with a grim smile, "when old Doc Fredricks said I got off with no injuries he wasn't quite right. He missed something. One of those trinkets I brought back from Vietnam got knocked out of its resting place."

Jan's eyes had gone wide, the pupils dilated until they almost obscured the blue of her irises. Her fear was no longer of the vague, nameless variety. Nick still carried two pieces of shrapnel from a shell that had exploded barely a dozen yards from him while he was accompanying a squad of Rangers on a reconnaisance mission. The most potentially lethal of the fragments, a narrow, wafer-thin, razor-sharp sliver of metal, was solidly wedged between two of his cervical vertebrae—or it had been, for the past several years.

"Where?" she whispered in dread.

"It's the biggie. The one in my neck," he answered, holding her eyes. "Ever since the wreck it's been slowly but surely working its way in toward my spinal cord. At least so I've been told by no less than three high-priced neurosurgeons who ought to know what the hell they're talking about."

"Oh, my God! Nick! How long have you known?" Jan's voice quavered, steadied, and then started to shake again. She was suddenly bone cold, and though she didn't realize it, she was gripping his hands so hard that her nails dug into his palms.

"About a month," he answered steadily.

"A *month*! You've known that long, and you didn't tell me!"

"I didn't want to worry you. Remember that trip I took to Houston, when I said I was going to meet an old crony from my UPI days? There was no old crony. I did see two specialists, though. The second one repeated almost verbatim what the first had said. Then last week I got the same speech from a guy in New York."

Nick sat there, looking at her steadily, and for a moment or two Jan had the half-hysterical sensation that this was all a bad dream. It wasn't really happening; she wasn't really hearing these things. And then she knew with a sudden, sickening terror that it *was* real. She drew a shaky breath and sat up straight on the sofa.

"Surgery?" she asked in a voice muted by fear of the answer. "Couldn't they...?"

"They all three pushed for it. I said no," Nick told her flatly. "And before you jump down my throat and demand to know why, I'll tell you. None of them could give me better than fifty-fifty odds that *if* I survived the surgery, I'd be more than a vegetable. I'm talking about total paralysis, Jan, from the neck down. I might not even be able to *breathe* on my own!" He paused a moment to control his voice, which had gone hoarse.

"There's no way I'm going to turn myself over to some knife-happy medic, with odds like that staring me in the face."

Jan didn't even try to argue with him. She knew that he meant it, that he wouldn't be able to face

such an existence—or at least believed he wouldn't
be able to, which amounted to the same thing.

"And without the surgery?" she asked, her voice
little more than a whisper. "What are the odds if you
don't let them operate?"

Nick's mouth twisted in a bitter parody of a smile.
"There aren't any. Sooner or later that piece of metal
is going to get where it's headed. When it does,
there'll be a lot of pain for a while, not long, and
then...nothing."

Jan closed her eyes, swaying with reaction, but
Nick refused to take pity on her and desist.

"I'll just stop breathing. Without oxygen, my
brain will starve, and then my heart—"

"Stop it! *Stop it!*" Jan's head was thrown back, her
eyes squeezed shut as if to blot out the image his
words conjured up. She tried to jerk her hands free
to hit him, to make him stop, to rail that it wasn't
true, *couldn't* be true; but he had her wrists in an
iron grip, as if he'd anticipated her reaction.

"*Janet!* No! Jan, stop it, now!"

His harsh voice sliced through her wild despair,
and Jan slumped forward as an agony of grief replaced the first hysterical, impulsive denial.

"No," she moaned. "No, Nick, no."

"Look at me," he said softly, lifting her face with
both hands. Jan didn't think she could bear the terrible sadness in his eyes. A tortured sob caught in her
throat as he held her face between his hard, warm
palms.

"I'm sorry," he murmured, and she saw that he
truly was, and that the sadness was for her, not himself. "I'm sorry, Jan. I wasn't even going to tell you.
If it hadn't been for meeting Marina in New York—"
He left the statement unfinished, his face taking on a
taut, set look. He closed his eyes for a moment, and

when he opened them again they were filled with steely determination.

"The plain and simple fact is, I'm going to die," he said brutally. "Maybe next year, maybe next month, maybe even next week. Now . . . as soon as you accept that, we can go on from there. Because I need your help, Jan. Not your pity or sympathy," he emphasized in hard tones. "We all have to go sometime, and God knows I've had a far better life than I deserved. I've always tried to fight my own battles, but right now . . . right now I'm vulnerable. You're the gutsiest broad I know, St. Clair," he said with a wry half smile. "I need somebody gutsy, somebody tough and strong on my side. Can I count on you to be that person?"

Jan faced him with outward calm. She would not burden him with tears, hand-wringing or mad wails of grief. All that could come later, when she was alone in the privacy of her bungalow. If it was strength he wanted—needed—then that was what she would give him.

"You know you can," she told him huskily. "I'll do anything you ask of me, Nick. Anything."

His relief was obvious, making it just a little easier for her to bear the pain. He released her hands and sat back, the tension almost visibly draining out of him.

"All right then," he said calmly. "It's Marina. For some reason known only to her, she's taken it into her head that we should get back together. You know I don't have any family—no parents, no brothers or sisters, not even a distant cousin. I have nobody to support, no hangers-on to create a steady drain on my resources. She knows that, too. I suspect it's got a lot to do with this sudden yearning for a reconciliation. Her career's not going well: she hasn't made a film in almost two years, and the last one was a monumental flop. Meanwhile, my last three books have all been million-sellers. Beginning to get the picture?''

Jan nodded grimly. ''She's a money-grubbing bitch.''

Nick's brows quirked in amused surprise. ''Crudely put, perhaps, but reasonably accurate. The point is, she's capable of using every trick in the book to worm her way back into my life, and believe me, she knows them all. The thing that's got me worried is that when...when the time comes,'' he murmured with a swift sideways glance at Jan, ''she'll be lurking around somewhere, like some kind of scavenger. She wouldn't give a damn what *my* wishes were. I could find myself locked inside an iron lung for the rest of my life, while she has herself set up as custodian or guardian or something until my money runs out, and then who knows? Frankly, the possibility scares the hell out of me,'' he admitted grimly. ''The possibility that she'll somehow manage to take control from me—not just control of my life, but control of my death. And she'd do it, without a qualm. It would be just like her to park me in the bedroom and then parade her latest stud in to entertain me.''

Jan was shocked and horrified, both by his words and by the savage bitterness in his voice.

''You make her sound like some kind of monster,'' she whispered.

''She is,'' Nick said in a flat, hard voice. ''The worst kind of monster there is—a completely ruthless, conscienceless woman. I can't afford to have her messing around with my life again for whatever weird kicks it gives her. I *won't* have it!''

''But how can you stop her? It's a free country, Nick. If she decides to come out here and try to convince you to resume your relationship, what can you do?'' Jan pointed out reasonably.

Several minutes passed before Nick answered. He just sat looking at her, his eyes narrowed to hide the expression in them. Finally he sat forward and reached for one of her hands.

"There's only one way I can think of," he said slowly. "A few minutes ago, you said you'd do anything I asked of you. Did you mean that, Jan?"

"Of course I did! You shouldn't have to ask that!"

"Okay, then," he murmured with a weary sigh. "What I'm asking is that you marry me."

2

THERE HAD BEEN only one possible answer, of course. Jan had known that even as she stared at him, mute with astonishment and afraid to trust her own hearing. In the ten seconds or so it took to recover from the shock, a glorious new world opened to her. Nick's wife! She would be Nick's wife!

"Jan?"

Her eyes focused on his face. He was frowning.

"I'm sorry," she murmured, then gave a small shake of her head. "You took me by surprise."

"Will you do it?" He watched her intently, and she could feel his tension in the lean fingers gripping hers.

"Yes. Of course." She was amazed at how calm she sounded. He might have just asked if she'd sew a button on his shirt or get him another can of beer.

"It would have to be soon," he said softly. He left the reason unsaid, but it hung in the air between them like a dark, ominous cloud.

"Yes. Fine," Jan agreed. The sooner the better. She wanted as many days—and nights—with him as she could have. She suddenly smiled. "Mom and dad will be thrilled—especially dad. He's always wished you were his son."

That coaxed a brief answering smile from Nick, but it died quickly as his eyes became solemn, almost grave.

"I want you to be sure about this, Jan. Very sure,"

he stressed. "Do you want some time to think it over?"

She shook her head. "No, I don't need to think it over," she assured him quietly. At the same time she was thinking, *If you only knew I've been thinking about it for fifteen years....* "How long will everything take—the blood tests and the license? Have you checked?"

Nick nodded. "We should be able to get everything done by next Wednesday. We could have a justice of the peace perform the ceremony right in the county clerk's office when we pick up the license."

He suddenly grimaced. "I hadn't realized how cold-blooded it would all sound. I'm sorry, Jan. You deserve better. You've probably always dreamed of a church wedding, with a white satin gown and a six-tiered cake—the whole bit. I'm being incredibly selfish to even ask this of you."

"Don't be silly," Jan scoffed. "Do you hear me complaining? Besides, all that fancy stuff could take weeks to arrange." She kept her voice brisk, deliberately skimming over the time factor. Actually, she'd given up her dreams of a big church wedding the day he'd married Marina Calhoun. But she could hardly tell him that.

Nick sank back on the sofa, closing his eyes on a sigh. "You've got a point," he admitted wearily. "Besides, you can still have all that later. After all, this marriage won't last for the rest of your life. Someday a handsome young devil will come along and sweep you off your feet, and you can have your fancy wedding then."

Jan was thankful his eyes were closed so he couldn't see her reaction before she got it under control.

"You're probably right," she murmured huskily.

Nick suddenly turned his head to look at her, his gaze direct and intense. "And when that day comes, Jan, you won't be carrying any emotional baggage to spoil it," he said in an unexpectedly grim tone. "I won't do that to you—leave you with unwanted memories. This will be a marriage in name only. I won't expect you to share my bed, or even this house if you'd rather stay in your bungalow. That way—" he abruptly turned away again, his jaw hard with determination "—when you do find the man you want to spend the rest of your life with, you won't have my ghost hanging over your head—or intruding in your bed," he added harshly.

The entire conversation had been unreal, Jan thought as she lay awake into the wee hours of the morning. She relived it all, dry-eyed now, with a sense of having been a witness, not a participant. It was the strangest feeling. Perhaps it *had* all been a dream, she thought in bemusement as she finally slipped into a heavy, exhausted sleep.

BUT IT HADN'T BEEN A DREAM, any of it. The following Wednesday she stood in what was to be her bedroom—or so Nick thought—in the main house, admiring the plain gold band on her finger. Janet Alexander. Mrs. Nicholas Richmond Alexander. It had a nice sound to it, she decided as she repeated her new name with a soft smile.

Then she reluctantly put her happy anticipation on hold and began to implement her plan. There wasn't much time. Nick was in the room he'd converted to an office, on the phone to New York. Jan knew from past experience that the call might last anywhere from two minutes to two hours, and she had a lot to do.

She removed the pale peach suit she'd worn to be married in, smoothing the material lovingly as she arranged it on a hanger, and then quickly dressed in old jeans and a plaid shirt. In just under half an hour she'd moved all her things into the master bedroom and stored them neatly away, out of sight. As she took a quick last look around to be sure she hadn't left anything lying in view, she felt a return of the anxiety she'd lived with ever since she had made her decision. How would he react? What would he say when she let him know she wasn't content to settle for a marriage "in name only"? Would he order her back to the other room?

Jan's mouth thinned as she stiffened both her spine and her resolve. Just let him try! She wasn't a St. Clair for nothing. She'd inherited her father's hardheaded Yankee stubbornness and determination. In all her life, the only thing she'd ever wanted and failed to get was Nick Alexander. Well, she had him now, and if he thought she'd be willing to play the part of his wife without enjoying all the benefits that went with the job, he could darned well think again! Her courage somewhat bolstered, she turned smartly on her heel and left the room.

They had been married late that afternoon, then stayed in town to have dinner at a fashionable steak house. Jan suspected that Nick was making an effort to bring some small amount of festivity to the day, for her sake. Either that or he just dreaded returning to the house they'd now be sharing. She knew him well enough to sense the guilt he was already feeling, and she also knew that he was not looking forward to the phone call they'd make together later, to inform her parents of their marriage. Nick was many things—not all of them admirable—but it was not in his nature to deliberately lie or deceive. Evan

St. Clair was probably the best friend he'd ever had, and Jan understood perfectly his aversion to acting the part of the happy bridegroom for her father. But much as he might abhor such a deception, he would be unwilling to burden her parents with his true reasons for marrying their daughter. Jan sympathized with Nick's struggle between loyalty and honesty, but she could think of nothing to say that wouldn't make matters worse.

As she passed the door to his office she saw that he was still on the phone. Nick flashed a rueful grin and held up his hand, fingers splayed to indicate he'd be finished in five more minutes. Jan nodded and went on to the living room, placed one of her Juice Newton albums on the turntable, then poured them each a glass of white wine. Nick joined her just as Judy Kay began crooning "Break It to Me Gently," her slight country twang imparting even more poignancy to the lyrics.

"Appropriate," Nick commented as he sank down on the sofa beside her. He sipped at his wine, made a face, then got to his feet again. "I need something stronger than this."

Jan stayed where she was and tried not to be hurt by his attitude. She'd known exactly what to expect when she agreed to marry him, she told herself firmly. He wasn't madly in love with her, after all; why should he behave any differently toward her now than he had for the past three years?

"Mom and dad should have finished dinner by now," she said casually. "Why don't we go ahead and call and get it over with?"

Nick tossed off a hefty shot of Scotch, sloshed more into his glass, and muttered, "Sure. Might as well spread the glad tidings."

He didn't move away from the bar until he'd

taken another swallow and replenished his supply again, but Jan didn't wait for him. She lifted the phone onto her lap and began to dial. He rejoined her just as she finished, and Jan gave him a soft smile of encouragement.

"In case I didn't mention it before, you look very handsome."

He hadn't changed out of the dark blue pin-striped suit he'd worn into town. With it, he wore a pearl-gray silk shirt and a navy-and-maroon-striped tie. He never bothered much with clothes, and she knew these had come off a rack, but they fit as if they'd been tailor-made for him.

Nick shrugged uneasily and reached up to yank the knot of his tie down a couple of inches, then unfastened the top two buttons of his shirt and took another swallow of Scotch.

"I told you how beautiful you looked today, didn't I?" he said with an anxious frown. "If I didn't, I meant to. You made a lovely bride." His mouth thinned as if he'd offended himself with that last remark, and he muttered a disgusted oath under his breath. "Aren't they home?" he asked in an almost hopeful tone of voice.

"It's ringing," Jan answered calmly. "And yes, you told me. Relax, Nick, it won't be so—Hello, mom! It's your favorite daughter. No, everything's just fine. As a matter of fact—Is dad there? Good, I've got some news for both of you." She turned sideways to face Nick, then impulsively reached out to clasp his hand. His fingers tightened immediately, and she smiled in reassurance.

"Yes, it's good news," she answered her mother's concerned question. "What best-selling author do you think got married today?" Her smile turned to a mischievous grin and she winked at Nick. "Right the first time—how did you guess? You hope she's not another what? *Mother!*" An irrepressible burst of laughter escaped her. "That's a terrible way to talk about your own daughter!"

She winced and held the receiver away from her ear a little, and the sounds of her parents' overjoyed surprise erupted clearly from the plastic earpiece.

"I told you they'd be thrilled," she whispered before placing the phone to her ear again. "Daddy, hi! Yes, it's true. Today—just this afternoon. I know, it was kind of a surprise for us, too," she admitted with a throaty chuckle. And then, in response to his next question, she murmured, "Happy doesn't say it by half, daddy," in a slightly husky voice. "Yes, yes, of course. Hang on a minute.

"He wants to talk to you," she whispered, her fingers curled to cover the mouthpiece. "He's so happy, I think he's about to cry."

"Oh, God." Nick sounded and looked thoroughly miserable. He took another hasty drink, then set his glass on the coffee table to accept the telephone. Jan noticed with pleasure that his other hand didn't relinquish its hold on hers; if anything, the pressure of his fingers increased a little.

He suffered first her father's jubilant congratulations, and then her mother's tearful ones, and thankfully neither of them gave him a chance to say much. But then Evan must have come back on, because Nick abruptly closed his eyes with a pained frown.

"Yes," he murmured in a voice that had roughened slightly. "So do I." Then he suddenly turned intent green eyes on Jan. "I swear to you, Evan, I'll do my damnedest to make her happy."

There was more. Her parents insisted that as soon

as their "honeymoon" was over they come home for a visit, but Jan uttered instinctive, automatic responses without really being aware of what she said. All her thoughts were optimistically focused on the promise Nick had made her father, and the look in his eyes when he made it. If he genuinely wanted to make her happy, it would take so little: all he'd have to do would be to let her love him, to accept the love she'd been hoarding for fifteen years.

As soon as Jan replaced the receiver he leaned forward to pick up his glass, then drained it in one gulp, falling back against the sofa in relief.

"Thank heaven that's over!"

"Oh, come on, it wasn't that bad," Jan chided as she replaced the phone on the end table. "Look at it this way—you've made two nice people very happy today."

She slid across the smooth leather of the sofa until their shoulders touched, one leg tucked under her. Longing to do more, she lifted her free hand— the other was still a willing prisoner of his warm clasp—and gently stroked an errant strand of hair off his forehead.

"Why are you doing this to yourself?" she asked softly. "It's ridiculous to feel guilty for marrying me. You asked, and I said yes. It's done all the time," she teased gently, as her fingers lingered to smooth the frown lines between his heavy brows. "The only person you set out to deceive is Marina, who deserves it. So stop sulking. You're starting to make *me* feel guilty."

Nick's head turned, and her fingers slid to his temple. "You?" he said in surprise. "Why should you feel guilty?"

Jan shrugged, a wry curve to her mouth. "Beats

me, unless it's because you're making me feel like an unwanted responsibility. Is that what I am—how you think of me?''

She knew better than to expect an insincere denial just to spare her feelings. Nick might refuse to answer, but he wouldn't look her in the eye and lie to her. So when he shook his head and murmured a soft but definite "No," she immediately smiled her relief, then impulsively leaned forward to place a light kiss on his cheek.

He recoiled. She knew she hadn't imagined it, but then he lifted his free hand to her face, tucking her hair behind an ear as his eyes held hers. There was a sudden charged tension between them, and as she looked into his eyes Jan was certain he was about to kiss her. Her heart rocked in anticipation, and her lips even parted slightly.

"You're incredibly beautiful," he murmured, his hand lingering to stroke the satin smoothness of her hair. "The first time I saw you, I remember thinking: by the time she's twenty, she'll have left a trail of broken hearts behind her a mile wide." Then his hand suddenly dropped and his voice took on a harsh note. "Yes, you're probably the most beautiful woman I've ever known, and I am definitely a flesh-and-blood man. But I made you a promise, Jan, and I intend to keep it. So do us both a favor, will you, and don't put temptation in my way if you can help it."

His fingers curved around her wrist and he deliberately pulled her hand away from his head, holding her eyes, his mouth a stern, uncompromising line. Then he stood up and carried his empty glass to the bar for a refill.

Jan's fingers slowly curled into her palms as by a supreme effort of will she forced herself to remain exactly as he'd left her, giving no sign that she was upset by his rejection. All right, so it was going to be even harder than she'd anticipated. Determination rose inside her, and she turned a composed face to him.

"Is it your intention to keep at it until you've emptied that bottle?" she asked coolly.

Nick threw back his head to finish off what was left in the glass, then shot her an almost defiant look before splashing more whisky in it. Jan noticed with a touch of disgust that some had slopped onto the top of the bar.

"It is my intention," he said slowly and deliberately, "to get as drunk as humanly possible, in as short a time as humanly possible—hopefully without having to endure a lot of sarcastic commentary from my beautiful new bride." He tossed off half the contents of the glass at one throw, then held it up with a mocking smile.

"Here's to you, Mrs. Alexander—one helluva gutsy broad." His words had already started to slur a little, and his eyelids drooped as he added almost to himself: "And too damn good by far for the likes of me." Then he flashed a crooked grin. "But what the hell—you're stuck with me for as long as it lasts. And while I'm at it, here's to as long as it lasts."

Jan rose slowly to her feet. Inside she was seething with rage, but outwardly she showed only cold contempt.

"You're behaving like an absolute jackass," she told him flatly.

Nick laughed. "So what else is new? Who but an absolute jackass would do what I did today? Listen, you want some of this before it's all gone?" he offered, waving the half-empty bottle at her.

"No, thank you," Jan refused stiffly. "It's been a long day. I think I'll just go on to bed."

Nick's tipsy good humor evaporated as he abruptly turned back to the bar to pour himself another drink. "Wise girl," he muttered. When he glanced over his shoulder, Jan had gone. There was a savage pain in his eyes as he swore softly and lifted his glass again.

HE INHALED DEEPLY, holding the breath in his lungs until he started to feel dizzy, then released it on a gusty sigh. His shoulders suddenly slumped. He looked like a fighter who'd already gone two rounds too many, yet knew that somehow he had to hang in there for another three. He felt even worse than he looked.

Could he do it? Was there the remotest chance that he could actually carry it off, keep up the pretense that he cared no more for Jan than she did for him? It had become increasingly difficult the past couple of months, knowing what he knew, and now that she was his wife....

His breath caught, his heart thumping uncomfortably as the word reverberated in his mind. His *wife*! He ruthlessly smothered his exultant joy before it could give rise to something even more dangerous. They'd made a bargain, and he fully intended to honor his part of it. His expression was grimly determined as he tipped the bottle of Scotch over his glass. Anesthetic, that was what he needed. Lots and lots of good ol' 120-proof anesthetic. Then maybe he'd be able to get through his wedding night without disgracing or humiliating himself.

TWO HOURS LATER Jan's nerves were strung so tight she felt like screaming as she paced the floor of the master bedroom, dressed only in a filmy white nightgown. *Damn* him! If he'd passed out in the living room she thought she might cheerfully bludgeon him to death with his own liquor bottle!

A heavy footfall in the hall made her whirl toward the door, her eyes wide. She barely had time to turn off the single lamp beside the bed before Nick's shadowed form loomed up in the doorframe, swaying slightly. He hesitated when he caught sight of her ghostly shape in the moonlight, then half turned, muttering, "Sorry, wrong room," as he started back out.

"Oh, no you don't!" Jan grated as she rushed forward. She grabbed him by an arm and swung him back around, and Nick staggered before he regained his balance. He'd removed his jacket and tie, and his hair looked as if he'd repeatedly raked agitated fingers through it.

"You've got the right room, Ace," Jan told him grimly as she grasped his other arm to help steady him.

Nick squinted down at her, then shook his head as if to clear it. "Jan?" he mumbled. "What are you doing here?"

One whiff of his breath was enough to make her back up a step in self-defense. He positively reeked!

"Nothing!" she snapped, already unbuttoning his shirt. "At least not until I've sobered you up. Hold out your arms."

Nick obeyed docilely, still peering down at her with eyes that didn't seem to be focusing very well. She peeled off his shirt and then started on his trousers, glancing up once to see how he was reacting to having her undress him. He didn't seem to be reacting at all. She quelled the urge to hit him—hard—and finished stripping him with a minimum of time and effort, making him hang on to the dresser while she removed his shoes and socks.

"What...?" Nick muttered once, then seemed to find the effort of finishing the question too much and fell silent.

"In here," Jan ordered sharply as she pulled him toward the adjoining bathroom. "Come on, Nick, I've had just about all I intend to take from you for one day!"

He flinched and raised a hand to shield his eyes when she turned on the overhead fluorescent light, but he barely had time for one resentful swear word before she was pushing him into the brown-tiled shower stall. Before Nick's anesthetized brain could suspect what she had in mind, Jan had divested herself of her gown and was inside with him, reaching for the cold-water control.

"*Sonuvabitch!*" he gasped when the icy spray hit him.

Jan placed herself between Nick and the shower head, seizing his shoulders to turn him full-face into the spray, and was rewarded with a stream of profanity the likes of which she'd never heard—not even from him.

"What the hell!" he choked when the freezing water had shocked his senses into stunned comprehension. "*Jan!* Good Lord, you're naked!"

"So are you," she replied tersely. "But not completely sober yet. Are you, Nick?" she demanded as she stared at him intently.

His strangled response was choked off as he quickly turned away. "For the love of— What the hell are we doing in the *shower*?" He turned back to face her on that last, complete exclamation, then sucked in his breath and spun around again.

"It was either that or hit you over the head with something big and solid," Jan answered, a snap in her voice. "And while the alternative would no doubt have given me a great deal more pleasure, I doubt if it would've done much to sober you up!"

The chattering of her teeth served as counterpoint to the caustic words, and when Nick heard it he turned to face her again. He was shivering, too, but there was a warning gleam in his eyes and his hands weren't gentle as they grasped her shoulders to move her aside. With a single, vicious twist he shut off the water, and then shoved her out of the stall with barely restrained anger.

"You stupid little idiot!" he grated as he snatched up a towel and flung it at her. "It'll serve you right if you catch your death of cold."

He turned his back as he yanked another towel off the bar and hastily wound it around his middle to cover his nudity. Jan's hands clenched on the thick terry cloth as if she intended to rip it down the middle, and a hot rush of anger put a halt to her shivers. Her mouth thinned mutinously as she crossed to the sunken marble tub. Laying the towel aside for the moment, she bent from the waist to wring out her hair, legs braced apart for balance on the tiled floor. Without completely straightening, she retrieved the towel and deftly wound it turban-style around her head, then turned to face him.

He was staring at her as if he couldn't tear his eyes away. Jan knew immediately and without a doubt that he'd been watching her while her back was turned. In one swift glance she took in his rapid, shallow breathing, the tightly coiled tension in his body and the way his hands were unconsciously clenching and unclenching at his sides. She deliberately planted her hands on her hips and looked straight into his stormy green eyes.

"Like what you see?" she asked softly.

Anger made her bolder than she would normally

have been. She'd had this night all planned—right down to the sheer nightie that had cost an arm and a leg and now lay in a sodden heap at Nick's feet—and he had turned all those carefully laid plans to so much wishful thinking with his drunken self-indulgence. Her eyes glittered as they held his without embarrassment.

Nick's jaw tensed at the provocative question. "You know damned well I do," he said hoarsely. Then he muttered a bitter oath at his own admission and abruptly turned away. "For heaven's sake, cover yourself and stop acting like some two-bit whore!" he rapped out in disgust.

Jan flinched. She couldn't help it. The words had been calculated to shame her, to make her flee in humiliation. For a moment she almost did exactly that, but then she realized what he was doing and a fresh surge of anger banished her embarrassment.

"Is that what I'm doing?" she murmured. "I always wondered how they behaved with a . . . customer." During that slight pause she silently crossed the space separating them to stand directly behind him. The points of her firm, upthrust young breasts teased his back, the only contact she allowed between their bodies. Nick jerked but he didn't speak. As for moving away, he couldn't. He was standing mere inches from the wall of the shower stall.

"Since you've obviously had some experience with that type of woman, maybe you wouldn't mind satisfying my curiosity." *Double*-damn him! She'd teach him to try to embarrass her! "What exactly would I do next, if I really *was* a two-bit—"

"Stop it!" The command rang out fiercely as he suddenly turned, his chest brushing hers before his hands clamped on her arms to roughly shove her back. "Just what in blue blazes do you think you're doing?"

Jan's mouth quivered at the corners as she answered. "I must not be doing it right, if you have to ask." His voice was harsh with anger, but there was more than a little confusion in his eyes, and that gave her the extra boost of confidence she needed.

Nick drew a furious, slightly exasperated breath and then glanced around for something to cover her with. His eyes lit on his own short terry robe hanging on the back of the bathroom door, and he snatched it off its hook and threw it at her impatiently.

"Put that on!"

Jan caught the garment with one hand and then dropped her arm to her side, letting the robe trail on the floor. "No," she refused calmly. She wondered if he might decide to put it on her himself, but apparently he had no intention of touching her if he could possibly avoid it. *Coward!* she thought scornfully.

Nick's jaw worked as if he was grinding his teeth, and then he abruptly spun toward the door. Jan was closer, and she beat him to it, placing herself squarely in the opening so that he'd *have* to touch her if he wanted her out of the way. From the raging fury in his eyes, she thought for an instant that he might do more than just touch her, but she stubbornly stood her ground.

"Why are you doing this?" Nick demanded savagely.

That question was one she'd anticipated, and she had her answer ready. "Because I want a real marriage," she told him, her voice steady and confident. "Not some farce where we live in the same house and sleep in different beds. I want a *real*, honest-to-goodness marriage, in every way."

"No!"

His reaction wasn't what she'd expected, and it threw her for a moment. The single, forceful denial had just seemed to explode from him. He certainly hadn't taken so much as a second to think about it. No, the response had been more instinctive than considered, Jan was sure.

"Why not?" she asked with a frown.

Nick exhaled an exasperated gust of air. "Why not?" he repeated angrily. "Why *not*? I made it clear from the start that I had no intention of sleeping with you, Jan, and I told you why not!" His eyes suddenly narrowed, his lips compressing to a thin line.

"More to the point would be *why* you've suddenly taken it in your head to try to seduce me," he said in a low, hard voice. "Have you already started to feel sorry for me, is that it—decided you'll make my last weeks or days as enjoyable as you can? Forget it!" he spat furiously. "I don't need or want your damned pity!"

Jan fought for all she was worth to keep a rein on her temper in the face of his idiotic male pride.

"Don't be a total ass!" she snapped, her eyes flashing. "Do I look like Joan of Arc to you? For pete's sake, if I feel sorry for anybody, it's myself! By now I'd planned to be spending my wedding night in the usual way, instead of which I've had to bring my brand-new hubby out of a drunken stupor, and *then* try to convince him I'm worth the effort it would take to make love to me!"

She saw from the sudden flare in his eyes that she'd gotten through to him, if only temporarily. Acting purely on impulse, she abruptly changed tactics, discarding her antagonism along with his robe as she took the short step necessary to bring her within easy reach of him. Now for the hard part.

Her hands lifted to his chest, resting lightly as she gazed up into his smoldering eyes. She held his gaze as she let her fingers start to move ever so slowly through his wiry, curling hair. Was she doing it right? Oh, please let her be doing it right. She had to rely on instinct alone, letting her love for him and an innate knowledge of what would please him guide her. Until tonight she'd never even *seen* a real live man in the raw, much less touched one; but there was no way Nick could be aware of her inexperience unless by hesitancy and uncertainty she showed him. With that thought in mind, she forced her hands to be more daring, running them up to his shoulders and then down again, past his chest to the edge of the towel around his lean waist.

Nick's hands flew to halt hers, his fingers seizing her wrists in an iron grip to lift her arms and force them away from him. His eyes blazed with anger and something else. It was that something else that gave Jan the courage to persist. He wouldn't let her touch him with her hands, but he was helpless to prevent the way she suddenly collapsed against his chest.

She felt his jerk of reaction as her breasts flattened against him, heard his harshly indrawn breath at the shock of her flesh meeting his. Jan pressed closer, rubbing her face against him like a cat, her tongue darting out to flick at his damp skin. Nick groaned and tried to push her away, but she let her arms and shoulder sockets take the strain and refused to retreat an inch.

"You're hurting me," she whispered against his throat.

"Dear God, you think you're not hurting me!" he rasped, but his bruising grip instantly eased and his arms fell to his sides.

"Jan, please." His voice was choked, thick and indistinct above her head. "You know what you're doing to me, damn you! Stop, before it's too late."

"It's already too late," she murmured as she yanked her hands free and whipped off his towel. Before he could stop her, she wrapped both arms around him in a fierce embrace. "Give in, Nick," she urged huskily. "If you don't make love to me tonight, I'll just keep after you until you do. I'll walk around the house without a stitch on all day, and sneak into your bed after you're asleep at night. When you're in the shower I'll come in after you, and touch you and kiss you until you can't hold back anymore and you *have* to take me."

"Heaven help me," he groaned, and she knew that she had won.

She stretched up, her mouth already open, and Nick's head swooped to meet her halfway. He reeled—that was the only word to describe it—literally *reeled* at her ready passion as she clung to him. But then he steadied himself, and his arms circled her at her shoulder and waist to crush her body to his in urgent demand, while his mouth greedily feasted on the sweetness of hers.

And then his head suddenly lifted, his eyes glazed as they burned down into hers.

"Why?" he muttered thickly. "I have to know why, Jan."

Something about him—a wary alertness, almost like that of an animal at bay—made her back away from giving him the whole truth. He wasn't ready for that; not yet, anyway.

"You really don't know, do you?" she whispered. A slow, seductive smile touched her mouth. "Nick, I've wanted you since I was old enough to know what it meant to want a man. I've spent almost half my life wanting you, and waiting for you to look at me and see a woman *you* could want. And you never even guessed, did you?"

He stood absolutely motionless as he drew a long, slow breath. His eyes closed as he released it just as slowly, a muscle in his cheek twitching once.

"No," he murmured, his voice low and rich. "I never did." When he opened his eyes, Jan was utterly stunned at what she saw in them, even more dumbfounded by the wry smile that tilted his firm mouth to one side.

"If I had, I'd've saved you all this sweat and toil," he drawled. "Because you see, my sweet little savage, I've wanted you since long before you had any idea what it meant to want a man."

3

FOR ONE WILD MOMENT Jan feared that her mind had snapped. He couldn't possibly have said what she'd thought she heard him say. Not Nick. Not to her. And then his voice, rough and strained with desire, laid her doubts to rest as he muttered, "And Lord knows I want you now."

And then his mouth was on hers again and he was sweeping her up in his arms, and all she could do was cling to his shoulders and pray this wasn't all a hallucination.

Her eyes were closed in ecstasy, and she trembled against him as his hot, open mouth worked its way along her jaw to her ear, where he murmured hoarse words that weren't really words at all, but rasping sounds of mingled pleasure and pain.

His arms fell away, but it was all right, because there was something else supporting her now. A bed, she realized dazedly, Nick's bed. Her eyes opened slowly, to find him there, leaning over her, his face flushed with passion and his eyes darkly intent as he gazed down at her. Jan reached for him, saying his name on a sighing plea, and his response was all she could have wished for — *had* wished for, countless times.

"Touch me, Jan. Make love to me," he urged as he pressed his lips to her throat and mouthed it roughly. "I've wanted to feel your hands on me for so long, fantasized about what it would be like."

The admission shot through her like a flash fire, freeing her to stroke and caress him as she'd ached to do for years. There was no shyness now, no uncertainty due to inexperience. She explored his body eagerly, avidly, learning how to make him gasp and moan with pleasure, her fingers alternately brushing delicately and kneading with passionate strength. She smoothed, fondled, squeezed, glorying in his feverish response; and all the time Nick was returning her caresses, repaying her in kind until need overwhelmed them both and Jan felt his strong thighs settle between hers as his weight descended on her.

They came together with an urgency that was almost violent, and Nick's harsh murmur of shocked surprise coincided with the soft little whimper Jan couldn't completely suppress.

"Oh, hell," he groaned into her ear.

Jan clutched him, terrified he was going to withdraw, leave her unfulfilled. "Don't stop," she begged desperately. "Please, Nick, don't stop now."

His entire body clenched, then shuddered, and she felt his throat work against her skin. She thought he was bracing to pull away, and her grip tightened to hold him.

"No," he muttered, his voice thick. "I can't. I can't stop." He lifted his head to look at her, and his eyes were tormented as he growled, "But, damn you, Jan—" The rest was lost in her mouth as his came down on it hard, in a kiss meant to punish them both.

Jan's instant, melting surrender turned punishment to reward as a husky moan of satisfaction whispered past her parted lips and into his mouth, and Nick trembled, his lips softening in contrition.

"I can't be gentle with you," he said raggedly,

without lifting his head. "Not this time. I've waited too long, and you've got me so—"

"It's all right," Jan whispered back against his lips. "It's all right, really. I don't care. Please, Nick, please!"

She soon discovered that he had spoken the truth; he was far beyond patience or gentleness. But she, too, had been truthful when she said it didn't matter. She surrendered to her own passion, letting it engulf her, fill her, until nothing mattered but the piercingly intense pleasure he was giving her. When they reached a simultaneous climax short minutes later, she could only wonder at the enormity of what had just happened, marvel at the frenzied response of her own body.

Nick still covered her, wonderfully heavy, his back rising and falling in a gradually slowing tempo as his breathing returned to normal. Jan let her hands run down his body with a deep, contented sigh. A fine film of sweat lay on his skin, and he smelled deliciously, gloriously male. She smiled as she rubbed her cheek against his hair, still damp from the shower.

"You little fool, why didn't you tell me!" he suddenly grated, lifting his head to stare at her in accusation.

Jan met his eyes steadily. "If I had, would you have made love to me?"

"Hell, no!" Nick snarled.

"Which answers your question!" she shot back. "And just why should you be so surprised? What did you take me for—some bed-hopping nymphomaniac?"

Her indignation caused Nick's lips to twitch in amusement. "Hardly," he drawled. He braced himself over her on his elbows, his eyes curious and watchful. "But a twenty-five-year-old virgin, in this day and age? Don't tell me there hasn't been at least one man you wanted to go to bed with?"

"Yes—one," Jan said clearly as she held his eyes.

Nick looked uncertain, slightly skeptical. "You don't mean to tell me you've waited all this time—"

"For you. That's exactly what I'm telling you." A smile softened her features and lit her eyes. "And though you haven't asked, yes, it was well worth the wait."

Nick hesitated a moment, then shook his head with a sideways quirk of his mouth. "Shameless," he pronounced softly.

"Is that a criticism?" Jan asked as her hands glided down his back to the curve of his spine.

He was smiling as he lowered his head. "No," he whispered, then claimed her lips for a slow, intensely sensual kiss, his hands moving on her shoulders with a deliberately light, teasing touch.

"And for your information, Pocahontas," he murmured as he eased his mouth from hers, "that was only the appetizer. The main course is still to come. But first—" he suddenly pushed away and rolled off the bed "—I have a little errand to run."

Thinking he was going to the bathroom, Jan lay and watched him, admiring the contours of his body and his masculine grace as he walked. Then she realized he wasn't headed for the bathroom, but the closet.

"What the...!" he muttered as he chose a hanger at random and held it up in front of him. Then, when he saw that he had one of her dresses, he laughed softly and replaced it in the closet. The next time his hand emerged, it held a pair of his jeans.

"Nick!" Jan sat upright on the bed as he started

pulling them on, not bothering with underwear. "What are you doing?"

He reached back into the closet for a shirt. "I have to run into town for a while."

"Into *town*! At this hour!"

"It's only twelve-thirty or so. I don't think they've rolled up the sidewalks yet," he replied, sticking his bare feet into a pair of scuffed old moccasins.

"Nick Alexander, you have got to be the most insensitive clod I have ever met!" Jan fumed from the bed. "How can you just get up and leave me after...after.... Oh, you pig! Go on then! Just don't expect me to be waiting when you get back!"

She started to scramble off the bed, but he caught her by an arm and pushed her back, then slid onto the mattress beside her.

"I won't be long," he promised. Jan glared at him, and his mouth curved in amusement. "Besides," he murmured, as he flicked a finger at her shoulder, "it'll give you a chance to dry your hair."

Jan's hands flew to her head, and she discovered that sometime in the last few minutes the towel had unwound and come off.

"Oh, no," she said in dismay. "I must look like a witch."

Nick laughed softly. And then, before she could let fly with a scathing comment, he pulled her into his arms and kissed her giddy and breathless.

"Don't pout," he chided against her mouth before he kissed her again. "It doesn't suit you. I'll be back before you know I'm gone. And you'll be right here in this bed, because that's where I want you to be. Right?"

Not sure she was capable of speech, Jan nodded docilely. He grinned and kissed her one last time, hard, then got up and left.

When she heard him return nearly an hour later she was sitting up in bed, her long legs folded under her. Her hair was a soft, shimmering curtain, which fell over her shoulders almost to the sheet, and she was wearing the gray silk shirt she'd stripped off him earlier. It gave her a bit more self-confidence to be covered, and besides, the slinky material still carried the musky scent of Nick's body. He entered the house by the front door, but didn't come directly to the bedroom. Jan scowled as she realized he was moving around in the kitchen; he'd sure picked a lousy time for a midnight snack, the inconsiderate swine!

When she heard his footsteps in the hall she scooted back against the headboard, trying to look nonchalant, if possible even a little bored. Nick paused at the door, his eyes unreadable at that distance as they traveled over her slowly. He was carrying a white cardboard box in one hand and two stemmed glasses in the other, and over his arm was slung—of all things—a beat-up old bucket.

"I'm back," he said softly as he came into the room. He placed the box and the glasses on a table beside the bed and deposited the bucket on the floor, then started removing his shirt.

Jan stared at him exasperation. "You're back," she said flatly as he sat on the edge of the bed. "That's it? You just stroll in and say 'I'm back,' just like that? If it's not asking too much, would you mind telling me where you've been for the past hour?"

"Not at all." Nick propped a foot on the opposite knee to remove a moccasin, then repeated the procedure for the other one. "I've been to a liquor store and an all-night bakery."

"A *bakery*?" The question was sharp with incredulity.

"Uh-huh. I got this." He picked up the box and put it on the bed between them, then carefully lifted out a small cake with the message: "Happy Bar Mitzvah, Stanley," in bright blue frosting across the top.

"Who's Stanley?" Jan asked with a frown. "And what are you doing with his cake?"

"Well, it's like this." Nick scooped up a glob of white sugar frosting with one finger and then sucked it off. "Mmm, delicious. Stanley's mother—one Mrs. Goldblum, by name—apparently decided she needed a bigger cake than the one she'd ordered, so they had this one marked down to half price. I know it's only got two layers, but I thought if you could just use a little imagination.... Here, maybe this'll help."

From a corner of the box he withdrew a miniature plastic bride and groom, which he planted smack in the middle of Stanley Goldblum's bar mitzvah cake.

"What do you think? If you back up a little, and squint...."

Jan hovered between laughter and tears, incredibly moved that he'd made a twenty-mile round trip in the middle of the night to bring her a substitute wedding cake. She managed a shaky laugh as she shook her head.

"You idiot." She smiled into his eyes, loving him so much it was a physical pain. Nick's answering smile was warm and tender.

"What's in the bucket?" she asked huskily.

"Champagne, of course."

"French?"

"*Mais certainement.* But it'll take a while for it to chill properly." His tone was matter-of-fact as he replaced the cake on the table and stood up. "In the meantime...." One large hand went to the snap of his jeans, but his eyes were boring into hers, and there was nothing casual or matter-of-fact about the look in them.

"The main course?" Jan guessed as she recognized that look and her heart set up a furious clamoring in her breast.

"Plus dessert," Nick confirmed in a throaty growl. He shucked his jeans and climbed onto the bed. "Now take off that damn shirt."

Jan shook her head. "You take it off. I've undressed you once tonight—now it's your turn."

"Twice," Nick corrected as he reached for her. "If you count the towel."

Sometime later, when she'd regained enough strength to move, Jan wriggled up on an elbow, leaning her other arm on his chest. "Tell me about when you first decided you wanted me."

Nick's smile was indulgent as he lifted her hair behind her ears, out of the way. "It wasn't so much a decision as a bolt out of the blue. I just looked at you one day and had this overwhelming urge to drag you down on the floor and jump your bones, right there in your parents' living room. You were fifteen, I think."

"Fifteen! Good grief, Nick, I wasn't allowed to even *date* until I was sixteen!" And then, as another thought occurred, she squawked, "And you were married!"

"If you could call it that," he muttered, grimacing slightly.

"You stayed together for four years," Jan pointed out with a pang of jealousy.

Nick shrugged. "More out of habit than anything else. I was so wrapped up in my writing, and she was hardly ever around, anyway. There were times

I'd forget I *was* married for weeks on end, until she'd come back from a movie location or one of her jet-setting jaunts with that Hollywood crowd.''

Then he suddenly whipped his arms around her and rolled, pinning her under him.

''And that's more than enough on that subject,'' he said firmly. ''We can surely find better things to do on our wedding night than discuss my disastrous and best-forgotten first marriage.''

''What was she like in bed?'' Jan asked solemnly, and he gave an exasperated snort.

''For pity's sake, Janet!''

''Well, you can't blame me for being curious. I'll bet she was a lot better than me, a lot more experienced,'' she muttered with a frown.

Nick's mouth remained firm, but there was a smile in his eyes as he leaned close to whisper, ''More experienced, definitely. But better—no way. There has never been anyone better than you in the entire history of the human race.''

Jan's eyes glowed as she clasped his head and pulled him down for a lingering kiss. ''We aim to please,'' she whispered, stroking his thick hair with loving hands.

''And to think I've spent the past ten years fighting to keep my hands off you!'' Nick said with a grin. ''You've caused me many a sleepless night, Pocahontas, but no more.''

''Not for the same reason, at least,'' Jan agreed mischievously.

''No.''

His voice was suddenly hoarse, and as they stared deep into each other's eyes, all humor vanished. Nick's hands moved to her head, his fingers restless in her hair.

''Jan, Jan,'' he murmured achingly. ''Sweet heaven, I want you again. I can't get enough of you. You're in my blood, like a fever."

"And you're in mine," Jan confessed as she instinctively moved beneath him, inviting possession.

It was true, she thought as his mouth locked on hers with a smothered groan. They were both burning up, his skin as hot under her hands as she knew hers must be under his. It was as if the figurative fire of passion was a literal flame, heating their blood and their flesh, consuming will and reason and reducing both to ashes in its fierce inferno.

As the sun came up they fed each other cake and sipped champagne, silently touching, stroking and caressing with fingers and lips until Nick took her glass and set it and his aside, then pulled her down in the bed. This time their lovemaking was slow and sweet, a leisurely, incredibly sensual voyage of discovery. Each lingering kiss, each exploring caress, seemed to last a lifetime as they sought new ways to pleasure each other. It had been the perfect ending to a perfect night, Jan thought in exhausted contentment as she fell asleep with the hard strength of Nick's arms around her and the solid thud of his heart beneath her ear.

THE FOLLOWING DAYS were a time apart, filled with laughter and passion and unbelievable happiness, made up of stolen minutes and hours. Their time together was all the more precious because the bittersweet knowledge was always there, lurking at the backs of their minds, that it *was* stolen time, to be savored to the fullest. Each hour of each day might be their last, and they were both desperate to wring as much from every waking moment as they could.

They worked together in the small organic garden Jan cultivated behind the bungalow, Nick muttering in disgust as he picked off beetles and worms and crushed them under the heel of his boot. Jan laughed at him and he threw a slug at her, his snarl so comical it made her laugh that much harder.

"Why can't we just spray the damned things?" he grumbled as he spotted a fat tomato worm and gingerly picked it off a leaf.

"You don't mind eating poisoned food, fine. The next time you're in town, buy some spray," Jan replied as she bent over a squash vine.

"Well, we could wash it off, couldn't we? This is revolting!" he exclaimed as he ground his heel down on the hapless worm with an exaggerated shudder.

"Nobody's making you help," Jan pointed out. "If the big strong former war correspondent can't stand all the blood and gore, he can retire to the house until the carnage is over."

"Funny," Nick muttered. "Yech, I'll never be able to look a butterfly in the face again. I doubt if I'll be able to eat any of these tomatoes, either, come to think of it."

"I'll remind you of that when you're scarfing down homemade spaghetti sauce this winter," Jan retorted without thinking, then closed her eyes on a wave of pain so intense it almost brought her to her knees as she realized he might not be there to cook for that winter. Thankfully her back was turned, so he couldn't see the tears that spurted to her eyes or the way she suddenly had to bite down hard on her lower lip.

"Why don't you go on in and have your shower?" she suggested, her voice tight with the effort of controlling it. "I'll finish up. There are only a couple more rows to check."

Several long, silent seconds passed before Nick

murmured, "Okay," quietly, and then she heard his
receding footsteps as he walked back to the house.

He knew. Oh yes, he knew, she thought as she
angrily wiped her cheeks. Damn it, she would *not*
give in to the despair that tried to claim her when-
ever unwanted thoughts of the future took her by
surprise, intruded on her happiness. Today was all
that mattered; she had to remember that and not
waste time agonizing over tomorrow. By the time she
had worked her way down the last row of plants,
she'd managed to regain her composure. Acting
purely on impulse, she gathered up three live tomato
worms and, carrying them in her cupped hands, ran
toward the house.

When she tossed the green-and-black-striped
worms over the top of the shower stall, Nick's curses
exploded around her and reverberated off the tiled
walls. Her laughter **was cut** short when the frosted
glass door flew open to reveal him standing there in
all his glory, his hair plastered to his skull and a
fiendish gleam in his eyes.

"No!" Jan gasped when he stepped out, hastily
backing toward the bedroom. He had one of the
worms in his hand, and his eyes were narrowed
with menace as he advanced on her. "Nick, what are
you—"

His wicked grin was the only answer she got before he lunged, laughing demoniacally when she
gave a squeal of alarm.

EVERY COUPLE OF DAYS Nick went into town to pick up
the mail, and on his next trip Jan asked if he'd stop
by a supermarket and buy her some canning lids.
She was in the middle of cold-packing tomatoes and
making juice.

"Will do." He bent to give her a long, lazy kiss,

then drawled, "I can't believe how domesticated I've become in the past week," as he held her against him, his hands linked at the base of her spine. "Frankly, it's got me worried. Yesterday I actually caught myself flipping through one of your cookbooks."

Jan produced a look of horror. "Saints preserve us, can the end of the world be far behind?"

Nick's mouth twitched. "I saw a recipe for Black Forest cake that looked fantastic. Think we might try it this afternoon?"

Jan laughed up at him. "Sure, if we've got all the ingredients. Are you planning to add gourmet cooking to your already impressive list of talents?"

"No," he murmured, pulling her close for a warm, enveloping hug, resting his chin on the top of her head. "I just like us to do things together."

"Like this morning, you mean?" Jan teased as she nestled against him and hugged him back.

"You're not mad because I woke you up so early, are you? I couldn't help myself. You're so beautiful in the morning, with your skin flushed and warm from sleep, and your mouth so soft and tempting.... I just had to make you open your eyes and look at me. And then when you did, I just had to make love to you."

"Did you hear me complain?" Jan asked softly. Her eyes closed as she remembered how incredibly tender he'd been that morning, how sweet her name had sounded on his lips as he whispered it against her skin between soft, almost adoring kisses. For a while she'd been able to let herself believe he felt more for her than just desire.

She kept waiting, hoping, but so far he hadn't uttered the three little words she so longed to hear—not since the day he had asked her to marry him, and she didn't count that time because they hadn't been lovers then. If he said them now, the words would have a totally different meaning.

And Jan had vowed that she wouldn't say it until he did. She wouldn't risk making the declaration a burden instead of a priceless gift to be cherished. By coming to him so eagerly and shamelessly, she had obliterated his guilt over marrying her; she would not saddle him with regret and remorse for a one-sided love.

So the words "I love you" were never spoken aloud. True, they both often said "I love *that*," while making love, and Nick frequently told her he loved the way she made him feel, or loved to look at her, or loved a particular part of her anatomy, or her intelligence, or her sense of humor, or her "spunk." Jan sighed as she arranged the jars of tomatoes on the rack of her large cooker. If she could believe him—and she did—he seemed to love every single thing about her; but apparently the parts didn't add up to a woman he could be head-over-heels, out-of-his-gourd *in love* with, the way she was with him. She had pretty much resigned herself to the situation. What choice did she have, after all, she thought wryly. You couldn't exactly hold a gun to a person's head and force him to love you. And heaven knew she'd had plenty of practice at loving without being loved in return. At least she had more of him now than she'd ever had before, she consoled herself as she prepared the next batch of tomatoes...much, much more.

NICK WHISTLED CHEERFULLY as he pushed the shopping cart ahead of him down the supermarket aisle. Canning lids, canning lids. Aha, there the little devils were! Hmm, there seemed to be a choice of styles:

plain flat metal ones, and some fancier gizmos that were part plastic and had a "magic button" in the middle. Shrugging, he tossed three boxes of each kind into the cart. As he moved on he resumed whistling the melody of "Chances Are." A stout woman in a print housedress smiled at him, and he smiled back.

It was incredibly easy to smile these days. In fact, he didn't seem able to stop; his face kept breaking out in smiles and silly, simpleminded grins at the most extraordinary times. Another housewife passed him, nodding shyly, and he smiled at her, too. They both halted to peruse the shelves, and she gave him a long glance brimming with female wisdom.

"She's a lucky gal, I'd say."

Nick looked around in surprise, but they were the only two in the aisle. "Sorry?" he murmured with another friendly smile.

"Your wife. She's lucky to have a man who's willing to do the shopping for her."

He looked down and considered the number and variety of the items in his cart, then grinned to himself. "No, ma'am, I'm the lucky one."

"Just married, right?" the woman asked shrewdly.

His grin flashed again. "It shows, huh?"

"Oh, yeah. My Frank had that look when we were newlyweds. Still gets it now and then. I still say she's lucky to have you. I hope she knows it."

Nick chuckled softly and lowered one eyelid in a conspiratorial wink. "If she doesn't already, she soon will."

"Atta boy," the woman approved with a nod before she moved on. He started whistling again as he reached for a can of cherries.

When he returned to the house he was carrying

two bulging grocery sacks, which he deposited on the counter.

"Good grief, I only asked for a couple of boxes of lids," Jan remarked as she turned from checking the seals of the jars she'd already processed.

He removed the earpiece of his dangling sunglasses from between his teeth and laid them on the counter, then dived into one of the bags.

"Kirsch," he announced as a bottle appeared. "And cherries—the dark kind—and black walnuts, because they're my favorite, and two pints of cream, and...ah, here we are. For a minute I was afraid that cashier left it out of the sack."

The last item to emerge was an aerosol can of whipped cream.

"Wow, you really went all out for the cake, didn't you?" Jan commented dryly. "Funny, I never thought I'd be jealous of a recipe."

"Don't be," Nick said, as he began to shake the can of whipped cream. "*This* isn't for the cake."

It was a second or two before Jan reacted. Her eyes widened as they flew to his face.

"Nick?" she murmured uncertainly.

"It's for you," he explained, just in case she didn't get the idea.

"You're crazy," she whispered, but she did nothing to stop him when he started unbuttoning her blouse. She looked down at his nimble fingers and shook her head in disbelief. "Crazy," she repeated softly. "Nick!"

"It's low-cal," he said soberly, as if that made all the difference.

Jan bit down on her lip to keep from laughing, then abruptly spun around and began opening cabinet doors, closing them again after a quick glance at the shelves.

"Darn, I know it's here somewhere," she muttered impatiently.

"What? What are you looking for?"

"Peanut butter," she replied without turning around.

It was a moment before Nick's startled "Peanut butter!" came in response. "Jan...*peanut butter!*" He sounded as if he couldn't decide whether to be more amused or shocked.

Jan found the elusive jar in a lower cabinet and turned to face him. "At least you don't have to shake it up," she said with a straight face as she unscrewed the lid.

Nick was eyeing the jar with a dubious frown. "You'll have to use a knife, though."

"Oh, no." A slow, utterly wanton smile curved Jan's lips. Laying the lid beside his sunglasses, she stuck two fingers into the jar to collect a thick gob of peanut butter, then transferred them to her mouth, sucking and licking it off with sensuous enjoyment.

"Here, try some," she offered, and Nick's mouth opened to accept her fingers. His frown returned for a moment as he muttered, "It's chunk style."

Jan laughed as she put the jar aside, and then he placed the aerosol can on the counter beside it with a deep, throaty chuckle and they began to hurriedly undress each other.

LATER THAT AFTERNOON they lounged on the sofa in the living room, Nick half reclining with his legs stretched out and his bare feet crossed at the ankles, Jan lying with her head on his lap. An idle hand stroked her hair, still damp from the shower they'd taken together, as he gazed down at her with tender amusement.

"Hussy," he accused softly. "Have you no shame at all?"

"Where you're concerned—none," Jan admitted. She raised her hand in a teasing caress, up his bare stomach to his chest, where she tugged gently at his hair. "Would you rather I pretended to be shy and ran from you every time you get that gleam in your eye?"

"Heaven forbid!" he said with a laugh. He started to bend toward her, then stopped, his lips compressing slightly. "Come here," he asked instead.

Jan came upright at once, sliding back to sit on his lap. "What is it?" she asked anxiously.

Nick shook his head. "Nothing. Just a twinge." He pulled her to him, laying his cheek alongside hers. "Don't think about it," he murmured in her ear.

"I try not to," Jan told him as her arms twined around his neck. "I really do, Nick. It's just that sometimes—"

"I know." He inhaled deeply, then released a long sighing breath into her hair. "If I had a million years, I could never pay you back for all you've given me this past week," he said with quiet sincerity. "With anybody else, this time might have been a sentence to be served, but you've made it a celebration of life. You just give and give and give."

Jan was afraid if she didn't do something to lighten the mood she would end up in tears. "Well..." she murmured huskily as her fingers raked through his hair, "it hasn't been entirely one-sided. Now and then I have been recompensed."

"Mmm, now and then, huh?"

"For the odd moment, yes."

"Liar," he breathed into her neck, tonguing the vulnerable spot just under her ear. He chuckled softly. "We're like a couple of addicts—if we don't get our daily fix, we're ready to climb the walls."

"Daily?" Jan asked mischievously.

"Okay, so sometimes it's more like hourly," Nick conceded in amusement. His arms suddenly squeezed her in a crushing embrace, and he gave a deep growl of pleasure. "I wish I could do something for you, give you something, to show you what this time together means to me. Something special, for you to keep, after...." He trailed off, leaving the rest unsaid.

Jan closed her eyes and pressed her face into the side of his neck, willing herself not to cry, and as she fought for composure the idea leaped into her mind full-blown. The simplicity and the rightness of it stunned her. She pulled back to look into his eyes.

"There is one thing I'd like," she said softly, hesitantly.

Nick's expression was solemn, his eyes shadowed and intent as he murmured, "Name it."

"A baby. *Your* baby. A part of you and a part of me—a little Nick I could watch grow, and take care of, and tuck in at night."

Nick seemed to stop breathing. "Oh, Lord," he muttered, his voice strangled. He gathered her close, rubbing his cheek against her hair. "You really know how to twist my guts around. Do you mean it, Jan?"

"Yes. More than I've ever meant anything," she told him earnestly. "I want to get big and fat and waddle like a duck, and have you put your hand on my stomach and feel your baby kick, and know that the best of us both will be passed on to him—or her. I want that, Nick. I do!"

Her eyes were closed, and though her long lashes were wet spikes against her cheeks, there was a soft, almost Madonna-like smile on her lips. Her words had come straight from the heart, and in her mind's eye she could already see a small, chubby version of

Nick, with a mass of unruly dark hair and his father's beautiful green eyes.

"Jan. Oh, Jan." Nick's voice was gravelly with emotion as he pressed his lips to her eyes and then her cheeks. He trembled as he held her, moved beyond words. "You know what I think I'll do," he said when he finally lifted his head. "The next time I'm in town, I'm going to buy a brand-new collar for that mongrel of Allen's. If it hadn't been for that mangy mutt running in front of the car, I wouldn't have you here in my arms asking me to make you a mother. Or even in my arms at all, for that matter."

Jan smiled up at him, her love shining in her eyes in that unguarded moment. "Get him a bowl, too, from me. Maybe we could even put his name on it."

"That sorry excuse for a dog actually has a name?"

"Sure, all Allen's strays have names. I think this one's is Dawg." She spelled it the way Allen did, and Nick pulled a face.

"Well, that shoots that idea. I was going to suggest we name the baby after him."

Jan laughed and gave him a tight hug. "Aren't you being just a bit premature? There isn't any baby to name yet."

"But there will be," Nick whispered as he lifted her hair to nuzzle her neck.

"Yes," Jan agreed with a shiver of joy. She knew what he was thinking: the idea of taking any kind of precaution hadn't occurred to either of them since they'd been married. "I suppose I could be pregnant already, and just not know it."

Nick went very still for a moment, and then he moved one hand to tenderly massage her flat stomach. "Now that's a mind-blowing thought," he murmured, resting his forehead on hers, his eyes closed. His hand circled her tummy in a gentle, almost reverent caress before he suddenly opened his eyes and sat back. *"God!"* he breathed; and then he smiled, a smile so filled with warmth that Jan's throat felt constricted. The smile evolved into a low, husky laugh, and then he kissed her hard, the kiss in its turn stretching into many fervent little kisses against her lips and cheeks and temples as his arms wrapped around her.

"Would it be safe to assume the idea appeals to you?" Jan asked breathlessly when he shifted his attention to her ear.

"Mmm, it would be safe to assume that it thrills me beyond belief. But I don't think we should leave anything so important entirely to chance, do you?"

Without waiting for an answer he eased her onto her back, his fingers already busy with buttons and snaps.

"Definitely not," Jan agreed happily.

"And don't you think, just to be sure...." He trailed off, his breath shuddering in his throat when her fingers brushed his stomach on their way to the front of his jeans.

"Oh, yes," Jan said in a throaty murmur. "Just to be sure."

Which were the last coherent words either of them said for quite some time.

ON SATURDAY Nick borrowed a horse from Allen Whitlow, the young veterinarian and collector of strays who lived half a mile down the road to town. Jan packed sandwiches and a thermos of iced tea in her saddlebags, and they rode to the mesa where she'd been photographing snakes the day he'd returned from New York. She spread a blanket and unpacked their lunch while, under her anxious gaze, Nick looked after the horses.

Although Nick's property possessed not one but two deep artesian wells—providing more than enough water for a lush green lawn, Jan's garden and an Olympic-size pool—the land surrounding it was primarily rocky and dry. Riding over it at any pace faster than a walk was sure to jar his spine and possibly cause the shell fragment to shift position. When they reached the mesa and Jan dismounted, her taut muscles had given testimony to the tension she'd been under since they set out.

Nick, on the other hand, seemed loose as a goose. If he was in any discomfort, it didn't show. Nor did it affect his appetite. After wolfing down two thick roast-beef sandwiches and complaining that the tea wasn't beer while he drank half of it, he stretched out full-length on the blanket.

"Well! If you're going to flake out on me, I might as well go look for photogenic reptiles," Jan claimed as she collected her camera.

Nick gave a noncommittal grunt and settled his straw Stetson over his eyes. "Just don't go trying for any close-ups," he muttered, crossing his ankles and folding his hands behind his head. "From now on, the only teeth that sink into that luscious flesh had better be mine."

Jan grinned and snapped three quick shots of him before strolling off. When she returned, he was lying in exactly the same position. She stowed the camera and then stood looking down at him for a minute before she dropped to her knees at his side. She thought he was asleep until one of his hands reached out and found her denim-clad leg.

"Now that's what I call a thigh."

"My mother warned me about men like you," Jan said soberly as she placed her hand over his.

"Thank goodness you never were any good at taking advice."

He thumbed up the brim of his hat so he could leer at her, and Jan chuckled. Then the hat was tossed aside as he grasped her hand to urge her down.

"You're nothing but a dirty old man," she said as she stretched out beside him.

"And you love it."

His arm encircled her to haul her on top of him, and their legs twined in a tangle of denim and leather. When Jan encountered the unmistakable ridge at the front of his jeans, she moaned into his mouth.

"Nick!" she gasped when he rocked his hips suggestively. "For heaven's sake!"

"What do you expect from a dirty old man like me?" he murmured as he began to work at the buttons of her shirt. "And don't pull that shocked innocence number with me, lady. You know good and well all it takes is touching you. Sometimes just *thinking* about touching you. When I'm not making love to you, I'm planning to, or remembering the last time I did...how if felt to be buried in you, with those long brown arms and legs wrapped around me and that sweet pagan mouth driving me out of my mind. Do it to me now, Jan. Make me wild with that savage little mouth."

She was helpless to deny either him or herself, not that any such inclination was present. The thrusting motion of his tongue was a deliberate prelude to what would follow, a taunting promise that molded her against his lean, hard length. Still, when he began to guide her over him, she resisted.

"No, Nick. Let me—"

"It's all right." His voice was thick, his eyes heavy-lidded with passion.

"But the ground...your neck," Jan persisted anxiously.

"It's all right," he repeated. Then, a note of tenderness creeping into his voice as his insistent hands had their way, he murmured, "You worry too much."

A shiver raced up Jan's spine as their heated bodies fused and she heard his husky moan of pleasure. Bracing her hands beside his head, she leaned down to delicately trace his lips with her tongue.

"It's because I'm selfish," she whispered. "I want to keep you around as long as I can."

Nick's eyes opened to take in her flushed face so close to his own, her softly parted lips and the pink tip of her tongue showing provocatively between them. The green of his irises had darkened to the color of a forest at dusk, shadowed and secretive. But as he gazed up at her, Jan imagined she saw a silent entreaty in his eyes, a communication that went far beyond physical need, an almost anguished plea from the depths of his soul.

"Nick!" she breathed in alarm, but before she could say more his hand slid to the back of her neck, and a twist of his wrist had her hair wound around his arm like a rope. A second later he forced her head down and his open mouth fastened hungrily on hers, and whatever she'd been about to say flew right out of her head.

NICK FOUGHT to throw off the suffocating sense of futility, the choking despair any reference to the future brought on. It wasn't fair, dammit! It just wasn't fair! He needed time: time to make himself the center of her world, time to make himself *necessary* to her, time for the affection and sexual infatuation she felt to evolve into the mature love he yearned for.

Jan moaned softly as she bore down hard and at the same time tightened the strong, supple muscles that held him captive within her.

Nick's fingers clenched on the firm flesh of her buttocks, his control slipping another notch. He shuddered from head to toe, wanting her to continue the sweet, slow torment, yet knowing he couldn't last much longer. Yet he possessed neither the strength nor the will to alter in any way the exquisite torture Jan was inflicting. It was always like this for both of them — the one who assumed control had the other completely at his or her mercy. At least for a while.

When he set out to make love to her, Jan let him, becoming receptive and pliant beneath his hands and mouth, allowing him to guide her, to determine the extent and degree of her participation. He was aware that this uncharacteristic submissiveness was largely due to her lack of experience; she was learning from him, letting him tutor her in the subtleties and refinements of the art of making love. What she perhaps failed to realize was that the lessons were as enlightening for Nick as for her. Each time they came together he discovered new ways to pleasure her, and in the process increased his own pleasure until it reached an almost unbearable level.

She was an unceasing source of joy to him as she brought all the wonderful qualities he adored in her to their lovemaking: her enthusiasm, her frank curiosity, her willingness to commit herself without restraint, and—especially in the past couple of days—her single-minded determination.

Always a fast learner, she had become confident enough of her newly acquired skills to want to experiment, to flaunt her expertise and test the limits of her control over him. She had begun to take the initiative, boldly, with an utter lack of shyness or hesitancy, growing more daring as Nick's responses testified to the success of her techniques.

But there is only so much one man can take, after all; and following such unremitting ecstasy he inevitably reached his limit. As he gulped the hot, dry air, his hands shifted to her pelvis, his grip an indication of his intent as he prepared for a transference of command.

"No!" Jan protested.

But he was already taking over, lifting her bodily. A low moan escaped him as he let her slip back down. He luxuriated in the sweet, warm slide, his eyes closing to magnify the sensations bombarding his mind and body.

"Damn you, Nick!" Jan said above him. She sounded a little put out, but more than a little short of breath; and the next time his hands urged her up she didn't complain. In fact she rose on her own, then slowly rotated her hips as she sank back to meet him.

Nick's breath fluttered weakly. "Damn me some more," he invited. The words were a little indistinct, sort of blurring together. He increased their tempo and received at first grudging and then enthusiastic assistance from Jan.

"You fink," she panted. "You always do this."

His mouth tried to shape into a grin, but he couldn't quite carry it off. "You don't like?" He forced himself to pause for a second or two, his hands holding her down when she would have lifted herself again.

Jan muttered something under her breath, and then she suddenly fell onto his chest. Her breasts flattened against him, her heartbeat matching his thump for frantic thump. Her hands dived into his hair to hold him still while her open mouth fastened over his. Her tongue joined the assault as it plunged past his teeth, circled his tongue, scoured the roof of his mouth. He felt her fingers link at the back of his neck, cradling, supporting, and knew that even in her passion she hadn't abandoned her concern for him. The knowledge caused the muscles of his throat to convulse, so that for a moment or two he literally couldn't breathe. He swallowed the tears threatening to drown him as his arms locked around her and they rolled together. Consumed by love and a fierce, aching need to give her more pleasure than she'd ever before known, he didn't hear the piercing cry of the lone hawk wheeling majestically overhead. Seconds later two other cries echoed it, one hoarse and exultant, the other softer, but equally ecstatic.

THE NEXT SEVERAL DAYS were devoted to an exhaustive and exhausting study of sensual eroticism. They spent hours at a time in uninhibited lovemaking. Sometimes it was playful, beginning with a tickling contest or a nude wrestling match; other times they made love with a wildness that was shattering in its ferocity.

They seldom left the house, and both the television and the telephone sat unused and forgotten. Their absorption in each other was total, leaving no room for interest in the outside world. Now and then, when she found herself alone for a few minutes, Jan had trouble believing it wasn't all a marvelous dream. But then Nick would suddenly appear at her side or sneak up behind her, and prove all over again that the reality of his lovemaking was infinitely better than any dream.

Tuesday evening they were lying face-to-face on the living room sofa, nude, nuzzling and exchanging warm, lazy kisses in the languorous aftermath of passion, when the phone rang. Nick's mouth turned down in irritation as he raised up on an elbow to reach for it.

"This is a recording," he announced, and Jan clapped a hand over her mouth to muffle a giggle. He winked at her and went on soberly. "Mr. and Mrs. Alexander are too busy enjoying their honeymoon to answer the phone. If you have information concerning large amounts of incoming cash or the death of a loved one, a message may be left at the conclusion of this recording. Otherwise, don't call us, we'll call you."

He bent to kiss her mouth, the receiver still held to his ear. Then he abruptly lifted his head with a husky chuckle.

"Evan! You sorry old reprobate, how the hell are

you?'' Grinning, he settled down on the sofa and shifted Jan to lie on his chest. "We're both fine, thanks. Suffering from chronic exhaustion, but I believe that's a fairly common complaint among newlyweds. *Me!* Hell, Evan, it's not me, it's this sex maniac you raised! She's after me constantly, can't keep her hands off me. Why, at this very minute she's—''

He broke off in midsentence, his teeth clamping together on a hissing breath as Jan tweaked several of his chest hairs.

"You vicious little savage!" he muttered in pained surprise.

"That's my *father!*" Jan whispered fiercely.

"So? For pete's sake, how do you think he got to *be* your father?" Nick pointed out, then delivered a heavy-handed love pat to her bare bottom in retaliation.

"Sorry, Evan, I didn't catch that. Work? No, I wouldn't call it work, exactly." He grinned into Jan's scowling face. "Oh, you mean writing! I'm waiting for the page proofs of *Fowler's Rage* to come in, but I haven't started anything new. I've been devoting all my creative energies to getting my wife with child, actually. With any luck, you should be a grandpa this time next year.''

Jan turned her face to his neck with an embarrassed groan, and he chuckled in unrepentant amusement.

"Sure, she's right here," he informed her father cheerfully. "Hang on a sec.''

"You'll pay for this, Alexander," she promised as she accepted the phone.

"I'm counting on it, Alexander," Nick whispered in her ear. Meanwhile, he took advantage of the situation to start fondling and caressing her in ways that made it next to impossible to concentrate on what her father was saying, much less respond coherently.

He and her mother wanted to know when they were coming "home" for a visit. In between squeezes and nibbles and licks, Nick murmured, "Tell him we'll fly back this weekend . . . then tell him you'll let him know our ETA later . . . then hang up the damned phone."

Jan barely managed to relay the message and say a hasty goodbye before he was removing the receiver from her hand.

"Time for the payback," he said with a grin, as he reversed their positions, dragging her under him.

WEDNESDAY WAS THEIR ANNIVERSARY. They'd been married two weeks. To celebrate, Nick suggested they go into town for dinner.

"And dancing?" Jan suggested hopefully.

He groaned. "Janet Faye, you know I'm next to useless on a dance floor. I've got two left feet and no sense of rhythm whatsoever."

"Oh, I wouldn't say that."

She came up behind him as he stood before the bathroom mirror. He'd just showered and was preparing to shave. His face was half obscured by foam, and he had a bath towel draped around his waist and a smaller one slung over one shoulder. He hadn't yet combed his hair. It gleamed wetly under the overhead fluorescent. He looked magnificent, potently virile, sexy as hell. She wanted to drag him to bed and love him till he begged for mercy.

"Jan, I'm a rotten dancer and you know it." The words were muttered out of the side of his mouth as he scraped the safety razor down one lean cheek.

"True." She stepped closer, pressing herself against

the taut bulge of his buttocks. Thrusting gently, she murmured, "But your sense of rhythm is out of this world," as she reached around him to tug at the towel.

Nick calmly wiped away the last traces of lather with the hand towel, then heaved another sigh. "All right, dammit, we'll go dancing."

Before Jan could embrace him, he spun around. His hands cupped her bottom to drive her forward, at the same time lifting so that she had to stand on her toes. The breath stuck in Jan's throat, and if his grip hadn't been so strong, she knew her suddenly rubbery knees would have given way completely.

"But first I'd better practice my moves," Nick claimed, a devilish glint in his eye. "Wouldn't want to embarrass you in front of a crowd of people."

So much for making him beg for mercy, she thought as he whisked her into the bedroom and quickly rid her of her clothes.

She spent a lot of time choosing what to wear, and an equal amount on her makeup. She wanted Nick to be proud of her. She settled on a two-piece suit of navy linen. The knee-length skirt was pencil slim and the jacket simple, with no lapels or front fastening, nipping in slightly at the waist and then flaring gently to follow the swell of her hips. She paired the suit with a crepe de chine blouse in deep maroon. It, too, was simply tailored, but the neckline plunged to the valley between her unconfined breasts. She fastened a fine gold chain around her neck and decided that was the only jewelry she needed. Navy open-toed sling-back pumps with two-inch heels completed the outfit.

She didn't wear a lot of makeup, but it was applied skillfully to make the most of her assets. The blue of her slightly uptilted eyes was accentuated by three shades of shadow ranging from palest lavender to smoke; a fine line of kohl rimmed her upper lids, and a coat of blue-black mascara lengthened and thickened her already luxuriant lashes. The winging brows needed no attention. Her high cheekbones were treated to a light dusting of pearlescent blusher, and her fully sculpted lips gleamed with a deep plum gloss. She left her hair hanging sleek and straight down her back.

"Wow!" Nick exclaimed softly when she joined him in the living room. For a moment he seemed dumbstruck, then he came to stand in front of her, gazing down at her with a light in his eyes that told her all her preparations hadn't been in vain.

"Lady, I don't know where you came from or how you got in here, but you've gotta leave. If my wife catches us alone together, there'll be hell to pay."

Jan laid a hand on the front of his pale blue shirt, thinking she was glad they lived in a climate where undershirts weren't necessary. Then again, Nick probably wouldn't have worn one even in Antarctica, she mused as her finger splayed and she enjoyed the feel of his wiry chest hair through the fabric.

"Jealous, is she?" she asked soberly.

His mouth quirked in a smug smile. "Insanely. Wouldn't you be?"

She gave him a slow, provocative look as she stepped away to collect his sport coat from the sofa.

"If you were mine, I'd chain you to the bed," she said in a conversational tone. She handed him the coat, and then smiled.

"Damn, if I wasn't a happily married man—" Nick muttered as he pulled it on. A breathtaking grin lit his face as he took her arm. "But since I am, I guess I'd better see you to the door. Wonder if I could get the little woman to go for that bit about the chains."

They had dinner in a small restaurant frequented mainly by local people and lingered over a second cup of coffee, as relaxed and easy in each other's company as any other old married couple. Finally, when he could put it off no longer, Nick paid the check and they went outside to the Mustang GT, which had replaced the wrecked Mercedes.

"I guess you've got your heart set on going dancing," he said as he opened Jan's door.

She turned to him, already feeling disappointed. "Not if you really don't want to," she lied.

Nick reached past her to brace a hand on the roof of the car. He was very close, and very, very desirable. "Oh, I don't mind all that much," he admitted casually. "It's just that there are one or two other things I'd prefer to be doing with you right about now."

Jan ducked her head to hide a grin. "I see. Just out of curiosity, would those other things happen to involve the use of chains?"

His husky chuckle made the muscles in her abdomen quiver with reaction. "Could be. Interested?"

"Could be." She let her head fall forward to rest on his shoulder. "Tell you what. Take me dancing, and on the way home we'll see if we can find an all-night hardware store."

"You've got yourself a deal, Mrs. Alexander." The words were growled into her ear with a fervor that made her melt. As if he knew—and he probably did—Nick's arm went around her to pull her up against him.

"Feel that?" Jan could only nod mutely and cling to his arms. He moved his hips suggestively. "Come to think of it, maybe dancing's not such a bad idea, after all. I can do this all night, and nobody'll ever suspect they're witnessing foreplay set to music.''

Jan's fingers clutched his sleeves, and she felt his biceps flex in reaction. ''They might get a little suspicious when I keel over in a swoon,'' she told him breathlessly.

Nick's soft laugh was a little breathless, too, as he set her free, and there was an anticipatory gleam in his eyes.

The club he took her to was small, intimate. Jan remarked on its coziness as they were shown to a miniscule table that hadn't been designed to hold more than a couple of glasses and the candle flickering in a bowl of ruby red.

Nick grinned as his eyes swept over her. ''The way you look tonight, I didn't dare take you anyplace too crowded.'' Then he added lightly as he leaned forward to brush at an invisible speck of lint just over her left breast, ''Besides, I wanted you all to myself.''

Jan's heart squeezed painfully. Her eyes were soft and luminous as she told him, ''That's a lovely thought.''

''It's also true.'' When his hand reached for hers she gave it to him gladly. He slowly laced their fingers together, his gaze fastened on their hands, long lashes screening the expression in his eyes.

''You know, I'm really enjoying this honeymoon,'' he said quietly. ''Makes me wish I'd married you ten years ago.''

''Ten years ago I was underage,'' Jan pointed out huskily. ''And you were already married.''

Nick's grip suddenly tightened, surprising her. ''I don't like to remember that,'' he murmured, his tone gruff. ''I'd rather pretend that part of my life never happened, that I was as fresh and innocent as you the first time we made love.''

He was still looking at their clasped hands, thankfully. Jan struggled against the swelling, choking surge of emotion that engulfed her, threatened to overwhelm her. Did he have any idea what that admission meant to her? She had to say something before he guessed.

"That might have been a little awkward. We'd probably still be fumbling and groping. No, speaking for myself, I'm glad you knew what you were doing, Mr. Alexander. *Very* glad," she repeated softly, her fingers sliding against his in a sensual caress.

Nick lifted his head to look into her eyes, and Jan was warmed and encouraged by the tender glow in his. He raised her hand to his mouth to kiss her knuckles, never breaking the eye contact, and her heart knocked against her ribs. If he'd just give her a sign, just one little sign that she could tell him how much she loved him....

"Let's dance," he said softly, pulling her up with him as he rose from his chair.

Once on the dance floor, they were lost to everything but each other. Nick held her close, but not indecently close. Their bodies brushed and gently bumped together as the music led them, the contact never lasting long enough to satisfy their growing hunger for each other.

Her breasts teased his chest. At the base of her spine his hand hinted at an increased pressure that was never applied. Her hand crept higher on his shoulder, stopping just short of his bare neck, denying him the pleasure of her touch. His knee poked at the material of her skirt as if he wanted to wedge it between her legs. Her hip grazed the front of his charcoal slacks.

It took the small combo about eight minutes to finish "The Shadow of Your Smile." During that time the sexual tension had built until Jan was dizzy with it. When the music stopped she was torn between disappointment and relief. Fortunately, Nick's arm was snug around her waist as they returned to the table, so she didn't actually keel over.

After seating her, he moved his chair closer, giving her no chance to regain her equilibrium as he once more took possession of her hand and his leg rested against hers from knee to ankle. A waitress appeared, and he ordered a Scotch and water for himself and a glass of white wine for Jan.

"What are you thinking?"

The question came at her softly and silkily, catching her unprepared. Jan desperately played for time.

"I'll tell if you will," she murmured with a small, forced smile.

Their drinks arrived, granting her a temporary reprieve. But when she went to free her hand, Nick wouldn't let her. By now her heart felt permanently lodged at the base of her throat. What *was* he thinking? He kept watching her, his clear gaze intent and probing. Gone was the carefree lover she'd known for the past two weeks; now he seemed to have lapsed into the kind of mood that always settled over him when he was working—single-minded, all his concentration on his characters and their story. Except he wasn't working on a story, and they were the only two characters he'd concerned himself with lately. Jan gave the waitress a nervous little smile as her wine was placed before her and the woman discreetly withdrew.

"Wait." Nick stopped her as she lifted the glass. Jan's eyes questioned him over the rim, and he smiled. "A toast seems called for," he explained. "Let's see. I know, let's drink to honeymoons. Wonderful invention, the honeymoon."

When they'd each taken a token sip, he set his

glass on the table and folded his other hand around
the back of Jan's, so that it was completely enclosed
by his warm grip.

"What's the time limit on a honeymoon, anyway?" he asked softly, his mouth crooked in a
heart-tugging smile. "You're the trivia expert—how
long are we allowed to drag it out, according to tra-
dition and social custom?"

Jan lifted her free hand to lightly finger his plain
gold wedding band. She'd been surprised when he
hadn't objected to wearing one, but decided he was
probably only humoring her. That was okay. It still
gave her a thrill to see that mark of her possession
on his strong, tanned hand.

"I think," she began softly, "that it lasts as long as
the two people involved want it to. A day, or a month,
or—in my parents' case—twenty-seven years, and
counting."

Nick released a sigh, his lips twisting ruefully.
"Well, we won't have twenty-seven years, more's
the pity," he said, then gently cradled her hand in
both of his and carried it to his mouth, kissing each
fingertip in turn. Jan's vocal cords locked in a spasm
of pain at the reminder, but outwardly she remained
calm.

"But I swear to you, wife of mine," he said against
her palm in a voice that had roughened slightly,
"whatever time we do have is going to be wonderful. Glorious. The honeymoon to end all honeymoons."

He reached out, sliding one hand along her jaw to
raise her face to him as he bent toward her. It was a
soft kiss, tender and sweet and promising so much
more than the thrill of his lovemaking that Jan felt
giddy with hope. When he drew back, her eyes glittered moistly, longingly. She breathed his name on a
note so wistful that it sounded like a prayer. She

wanted him to take her home, to get them both out of this place, which suddenly seemed far too public and crowded, and hold her and stroke her and join himself to her while he whispered heated love words in her ear. She communicated all this to him with her eyes, and her softly parted lips, and the way she leaned toward him in silent supplication.

Nick smiled in perfect understanding, but made no move to leave. Instead he placed another gentle kiss on her lips and then sat back to look at her, seeming to drink in the sight of her, his green eyes dark and compelling as they wandered without haste over each lovely feature.

"You are so beautiful," he whispered. "So unbelievably perfect. Sometimes I have trouble believing you're really mine."

"I'm yours," Jan breathed, and he smiled as his thumb brushed the corner of her mouth.

"Mine," he repeated, savoring the word. "You said you'd tell what you were thinking, if I went first." His hesitation was brief. "What I was thinking was how lucky I am to have discovered you... us, what we have... before it was too late, and how very much I—"

"Well, well, if it isn't the newlyweds!"

The jovial remark cut short the rest of Nick's admission, or confession, or whatever it would have been. They both looked up—Jan in bemused surprise and Nick with an irritation he didn't bother to conceal—and found Allen Whitlow standing next to their table with a leggy redhead at his side.

"Hello, Allen," Nick said tersely. "You're the last person I expected to run into tonight."

"I could say the same, ol' buddy," Allen replied with a grin. He either ignored or was unaware of the slight chill in Nick's greeting. "If *I'd* just married this foxy lady, you can bet we'd still be holed up at home." Jan couldn't resist smiling at the exaggerated wink he gave her, and didn't notice the way Nick's mouth tightened in aggravation.

"Hey, remember me?"

Allen's head turned at the dry comment from his companion, and he grinned again. "Sorry. Lisa, these are my neighbors, the Alexanders. Nick, Jan, meet Lisa Selby."

Lisa's eyes widened comically. "Nick Alexander? *The* Nick Alexander, the *writer*? Oh, I can't believe it—I've read all your books...twice!"

Nick smiled graciously, but Jan could almost hear his inner groan. He was naturally grateful to all the people who shelled out their hard-earned cash to buy his books, but he loathed the visibility that went with being a best-selling author. His editors complained that getting him to agree to autograph sessions and book tours was like pulling teeth. Jan squeezed his hand in sympathy as Lisa continued to gush, and his fingers gripped hers tightly.

Somehow, without having been invited, Allen and Lisa appropriated two chairs and joined them. Jan had to squelch a grin at the exasperated look on Nick's face when he found himself sandwiched between her and the talkative Lisa, who, it turned out, was a journalism major.

"Wouldn't you just know it?" he muttered under his breath when Lisa allowed herself to be side-tracked long enough to place her drink order. "I'll lay you ten to one she plans to write the Great American Novel."

"You can afford to be kind," Jan chided close to his ear. "She obviously thinks you're the greatest thing since sliced bread. It won't hurt to give her a little of your time, pay her a little attention. She'll remember this night for the rest of her life."

"I don't *want* to pay her a little attention," Nick growled under cover of a smile. "I want to pay *you* a *lot* of attention." His hand dropped to her thigh and squeezed gently. "And I don't have to tell you what kind of attention I have in mind, do I?"

"No," Jan breathed, her eyelids drooping and her hand surreptitiously closing over his. His moan was so low only she could have heard it.

"When you go all soft and dreamy like that, I—"

Lisa turned to him again at that moment, and Jan thought it was probably a good thing. Another few seconds, and they'd have been sliding under the table to make love on the floor.

Allen didn't seem concerned that his date was virtually ignoring him. While she fawned over Nick, Allen drew Jan into a conversation about her photography. He'd often encouraged her to submit some of her pictures to the natural history or wildlife magazines, or even consider publishing them in a coffee-table book of her own. While his praise and encouragement were flattering, Jan had never given serious consideration to either idea. Frankly, she doubted her work was good enough.

As Allen insisted that it was and pressed her to at least submit some of her photos, she laughed at his perseverance, becoming more and more animated as he cajoled and lavished extravagant compliments on her. They were both chuckling when Allen suddenly sprang to his feet.

"Hey, they're playing 'Wipeout'! Come on, Jan, let's see if we've lost our touch."

She was dragged out of her chair and onto the dance floor, and by the time they returned to the table, both were panting from the exertion.

"Whew! That'll flat take it out of you!" Allen claimed breathlessly.

"You're just getting old," Lisa teased.

"Old! I'll have you know I'm a good five or six years younger than Nick, there."

"I'd never have guessed," Lisa answered. She smiled adoringly up at Nick, who was looking grimmer by the minute. Concern banished Jan's enjoyment of the friendly banter as she wondered if he might be in pain.

"Well," he said, abruptly rising to his feet, "this old geezer's calling it a night. I'm not worth a plug nickel if I don't get my eight hours, right, ma?"

Jan smiled, but she was disturbed by both his set expression and the brusqueness of his voice.

"All right, then go," Allen said genially. "But first...." Jan was taken by surprise when he suddenly wrapped both arms around her. "I just realized I haven't kissed the bride yet."

He planted an enthusiastic kiss smack on her mouth, then held her away and smiled into her eyes. "Be happy, sweetheart," he said softly.

His sincerity touched her. She impulsively hugged his neck. Allen had been a good friend to her over the past three years, and it was nice to know her marriage wouldn't change that.

"I already am," she said truthfully as she released him. "Good night, Lisa. It was nice meeting you."

Nick was silent all the way home, and Jan sensed that his mind was occupied with something other than driving. When they reached the house, she hesitated in the living room. If something was bothering him, or if he was experiencing any discomfort, she wanted to know about it. But he moved past her toward the bar, shrugging out of his jacket on the way. He tossed it over the back of the sofa and reached for a bottle of Scotch.

"Nick?" she said tentatively. "What's wrong?"

"Nothing's wrong," he answered quietly, not turning to face her. "Why don't you go on to bed? I'll be along in a minute."

She was tempted to stay and force the issue, but something about the set of his shoulders, the quiet determination in his voice, made her murmur a soft "Okay," and turn for the hall instead.

She was in bed, covered by a single sheet, when he finally came in. He had a drink in his hand, Jan noticed anxiously. Instead of starting to undress, or heading for the bathroom, he came to her side of the bed and stood looking down at her for a long, silent few seconds. Then he finished off the liquor in his glass and set it on the night table with a force that was all the more noticeable for being restrained.

"We have to talk," he said without preamble.

"All right." Jan sat up and scooted toward the middle of the bed, patting the mattress beside her in invitation.

He sank onto it, but didn't offer to take the hand she left lying close to his hip, or touch her in any way. Jan searched his face for a clue as to what was bothering him, but there was nothing; his expression was closed, shuttered, denying her access to his thoughts or feelings. She sat back with a sigh to wait for him to enlighten her.

"I'm going to ask you something, and I want you to be absolutely truthful with me." He sounded as if he was reciting a memorized speech. Had he been rehearsing this?

Jan frowned slightly. "All right," she said again. "What do you want to know?"

Nick hesitated, and she had the absurd feeling that he was afraid, that he dreaded both the question and the answer. Panic leaped to life inside her. He'd guessed. She'd somehow given herself away. He was going to ask if she was in love with him, and when she told him the truth it would drive him away from her for good. Her hands felt clammy, and her breathing became shallow and rapid as every muscle in her body tensed for the rejection she knew was about to come.

He cleared his throat softly. He glanced toward the empty glass, as if wishing he'd left a little whisky, and then his mouth tightened and he turned back to look her straight in the eye.

"What does Allen Whitlow mean to you?"

The words rapped out one right after the other, a challenge, an accusation, almost. Jan's relief was so great she thought it was a good thing she was already sitting on the bed, or she might have collapsed. Then, on the heels of the relief, came an indescribable joy. He was *jealous*! Miracle of miracles, he was actually jealous, of Allen! The hardest thing she'd ever had to do in her life was to remain relaxed against the pillows and face him calmly, but she did it.

"He's a friend," she answered distinctly. "A very dear friend, but that's all. What did you think he meant to me?"

Doubt warred with gladness in Nick's eyes before he rose from the bed in an impatient move and took several restless paces away from her.

"You spend a lot of time over there," he said tersely.

"Yes. I told you, he's my friend. The only friend I've made here, really, except of course for you. We share a lot of interests—the respect for all living things, our tastes in music. He has a huge record collection from the fifties and sixties, and he likes to dance," she added, a soft, teasing note in her voice as she drew her legs under her in preparation for climbing off the bed. "You've never made any secret of the fact that you *hate* to dance. Sometimes when I'm over there, Allen puts a stack of forty-fives on the turntable and we boogie to our hearts' content. He's also been very supportive of my photography. I show him what I've done, and he gives me critical advice about how to improve the results."

While she spoke, she edged her legs from under the sheet and shifted to sit on the edge of the mattress. Nick kept his back to her, but she wasn't discouraged. Jealousy, she could deal with...gladly.

"I didn't realize he was such an expert on photography," he said gruffly.

Jan grinned behind his back. He was relieved, and embarrassed about it. *I love you, Nick Alexander,* she told him silently as she stood and the sheet fell away, leaving her gloriously naked.

Jan crept up behind him soundlessly, stopping a foot short of him. "I prefer your own special talents," she offered in a silky whisper. "As I said before, you've got fantastic rhythm."

She took that last step and wound her bare arms around his waist, and felt him tense in immediate response. Her hands glided lovingly up and down him, one reaching for the buttons of his shirt and the other seeking out his belt buckle. He pressed back against her breasts and neither hindered nor helped her.

"Jan, are you sure.... I mean, he's close to your own age, and as you said, you've got a lot in common. I couldn't blame you if you—"

Her hands finished their tasks in record time, finding his heated flesh and exploring it with an eager abandon that cut off both his words and his breath.

"Listen and listen good," she said as she caressed

and readied him. "If I had wanted Allen Whitlow, I'd have gone after Allen Whitlow. What's more, I'd have got him. Do you doubt that?"

Nick's head jerked in denial, a soft moan escaping him as both his hands clamped over hers.

"Good. I got the man I wanted, the man I've always wanted," she told him huskily, her strong fingers kneading and squeezing. "By now, there shouldn't be any doubt about that, either."

"Oh, Jan!" was his choked, gasping reply as he turned in to her arms and his closed around her urgently.

That night their lovemaking was the best ever. When he lay down beside her, he held her as if she was the most precious thing in his world. His hunger was tempered by the desire to give, his impatience moderated by fierce tenderness as he loved her over and over. They finally fell asleep for the last time near dawn, wrapped around each other in the center of the bed, the covers long since discarded and lying in a rumpled heap on the floor.

5

THURSDAY WAS one of those bright, cloudless days that bring hordes of tourists and asthmatics thronging to the Southwest.

Jan worked in her garden during the morning, while Nick made an effort to catch up on his mail. This group wanted him to lecture at a writers' workshop in Arkansas. That group had one scheduled for the same weekend in Illinois. A group of librarians invited him to address them on the subject: "The Dearth of Literacy in Twentieth-Century American Writing." An English professor in Terre Haute, Indiana, thought his students would benefit by a visit from someone "whose style they all seem to be trying to emulate," judging by the essays he'd graded so far this term.

At eleven he stood up behind his desk with a muttered oath, deciding to take a breather. He stopped off at the kitchen for a couple of cold beers, then left the house by way of the patio door, humming under his breath. Jan was washing her hands at the outside faucet. She looked up with a smile as he stopped beside her and held out one of the beers.

"Thought you might be ready for this."

"I am. Thanks." She twisted off the cap and dropped it into a small garbage can at her feet, then tipped her head back for a long swallow. "Mmm, that hit the spot. Are you goofing off, or have you caught up on everything?"

"I'm giving myself a much-deserved break, and at the same time using it as an excuse to spend some special time with my wife. Make that my beautiful, sexy, wonderfully lascivious wife," he added soberly, then chugged half the beer in his bottle at one go.

"Oh. Well in that case, why don't we get comfy on a chaise or something?"

"Terrific idea."

He took her hand and they strolled to a roomy redwood chaise beside the pool. Jan settled naturally into the curve of his arm as they stretched out. They were both wearing cutoffs and T-shirts, and both were barefoot. Nick lazily ran the sole of one foot up her leg to the knee, and then back down. His toes played with hers, and he smiled.

"Have I ever told you you've got fantastic legs?"

"No, I don't believe you have."

"Well, you do. Long and brown and perfectly shaped. Strong, too. I thought for a while there last night you were gonna break my back."

Jan gave him a repentant frown and sipped at her beer. "Gosh, I'm sorry. I'll try to remember to keep my legs to myself from now on."

Nick grinned, then drained his beer and deposited the bottle on the patio to wrap both arms around her. "When you told Allen you were happy, was it the truth?"

Jan smiled and nestled against him. "Oh, yes. I am sublimely, serenely, superbly happy."

He dropped a kiss on the top of her head before resting his chin there.

"How about you?" Jan couldn't resist asking. After last night she thought she knew, but she still wanted to hear him say it.

"Heaven no longer holds any mystery for me,"

Nick answered softly. "I've spent the past two weeks there. It's been the richest, most golden time... you've given me such joy. If it had to end now, with my next breath, I couldn't—"

"No!" The half-empty bottle dropped from Jan's hand to shatter on the patio as she turned blindly into his chest, her arms fastening around him in a desperate embrace. "No!" she repeated on a sob. Tears coursed down her cheeks, and she clung to him with a frantic strength. "I don't want you to die! You *can't* die! You can't leave me, Nick!"

The muscles in his arms convulsed, crushing her against him. "*Jan!* Oh, Jan, don't!" He took a moment to steady his voice, drawing a ragged breath. "Don't you think I feel it, too—the fear, the rage," he said hoarsely. "Sometimes it sneaks up on me, and I want to break things, smash my fist through a wall. I lie awake at night, watching you sleep. I've been trying to soak up every sight and sound while I can, all the time knowing it's not enough. Oh, Jan, Jan. I don't want to leave you, baby. Not now, not after these two weeks. Dammit, I want *years* with you, not weeks or months!"

Jan pulled back, her eyes swimming in grief. "Have the operation," she begged. "Call one of those specialists, *now*, and tell him you'll do it!"

Nick's anguished eyes held hers as he hesitated.

"Please, Nick!" She clutched at his shirt, desperate to make him agree, terrified that he wouldn't. "Give us those years. I want them, too."

Still he didn't speak. Throwing caution to the winds, she let him see the truth in her shimmering eyes while she whispered it with lips that trembled uncontrollably.

"I love you. Oh, Nick, I love you so. Please."

He stopped breathing, shock leaching the blood

from his face. For an instant out of eternity the earth ceased turning, time stood still, and Jan teetered on the brink of a yawning chasm as she realized the enormity of what she'd done.

And then he pressed her face into his neck with an agonized groan, his lips hot and dry as they brushed down her cheek to her ear. The sun shone again, her heart beat again, and the pain returned worse than before.

"Nick?" she whispered against his skin. It was a plea, an entreaty that he tell her what she so desperately wanted to hear.

"Yes," he groaned, lifting her face to let her see it blazing in his eyes. "Oh, *yes*! More than anything, more than I can ever tell you. Jan...Jan!"

His head descended to her, and as he choked out her name the second time, their seeking mouths met and fused. It wasn't one kiss they shared, but many small kisses—a dozen, two dozen—each achingly sweet and at the same time passionately intense.

"I love you, I love you," Nick breathed into her mouth between them.

Tears trickled down Jan's cheeks as she joyously echoed the words, free at last to speak them aloud. When they could bear to break apart, he held her face in his hands and told her with his glistening eyes. They were both trembling.

"Can it be true?" Nick said uncertainly. "I'm not dreaming, am I? Tell me I'm not, Jan."

Her smile was gentle, infinitely tender as she raked her fingers through the unruly hair above his ear. "You're not dreaming, darling, and neither am I. No dream could ever be this good."

The breath left him in a long, pent-up sigh as he gathered her to him, his arms gentle, protective and yet possessive, too. Jan hugged his chest, and tingled all over at the soft kiss he laid on her brow.

"You will have the operation now, won't you?" She was certain he would say yes; that no risk would be too great now that they were secure in each other's love.

When he didn't answer at once, she lifted her head from his chest, her eyes darkening with fear. "Nick?"

"I can't." The assertion was tormented, but filled with conviction.

"Of course you can! Nick, you just told me you *love* me, that you want years with me! We can have them.... All you have to do is agree to that operation!"

Nick shook his head. His eyes were dark with pain, and there was a ring of white around his lips. Jan couldn't believe he was still refusing. She stared at him helplessly.

"Don't you understand?" His voice was a hoarse rasp. "It's *because* I love you that I can't do it! Jan, please—"

"No!" He was begging for her understanding, but the only thing she understood was that he hadn't changed his mind—that he was prepared to die rather than agree to the surgery.

"You can't love me!" she cried, her pain too great to contain. "If you did, you couldn't do this to me, to us! Nick, I beg you, *please*! I don't know what I'd do without you. I'd want to die, too!"

"Don't!" His face had gone white, the skin stretched tight across his cheekbones. He grasped her shoulders cruelly, his fingers digging into her flesh. "For heaven's sake, Jan!" His throat worked convulsively before he could go on. "Please... you're only making this harder for me, and it's already tearing me in two. Can't you see that? Not love you! Dear God, if I didn't love you so much, it would be easy to say yes! But they've already warned me how the surgery might turn out. What if I came out of it a useless vegetable who couldn't even feed himself?''

"Do you think I'd care?" Jan demanded wildly.

Nick closed his eyes, his taut white face showing the agony his decision was causing him, and she knew then that nothing she could say or do would change his mind. She felt as if someone had hit her in the center of her chest with an ax.

"I think you honestly believe you wouldn't care," he said quietly, fighting to control his voice. "And at first, maybe you wouldn't. But *I would*!" He had to pause again, and then went on.

"And eventually, when the days turned into weeks, months, maybe even years, your love would turn to pity...and then resentment for the burden I'd become. We'd both be caught in a trap, a prison of our own making. Mine would be physical and yours would be emotional, but just as confining, just as embittering. I know you, Jan. You're as loyal as they come. You'd never leave me, and I doubt if you could even bring yourself to turn to someone else for what I could no longer give you." His voice dropped, sounding exhausted and resigned as he added, "And that's when the pity and the resentment might easily turn to hate."

"Never!" Jan breathed with unshakable conviction.

Nick's mouth twisted in a bitter travesty of a smile. "I wish to God I could believe that. But I'm a realist, Jan. I'd rather die once, while I know I still have your love, than every time I looked into your eyes and saw pity or regret or guilt."

She swallowed against the constriction in her throat, refusing to give up even when she knew she couldn't win.

"But it might not be that way. The doctors told you the odds—"

"Would be only fifty-fifty. *If* I survived the surgery."

He had mastered his emotion, Jan saw in despair. He was composed and determined, and her heart was breaking in two. She sagged against him hopelessly and his arms tightened, offering strength and comfort.

"I love you," he whispered into her hair. "Always remember that. No man has ever loved a woman as I love you. And you'll never really lose me, because the best of me is already yours, a part of you, and always will be."

For a while they just held on to each other, tightly, neither speaking nor moving. And then Nick's chest rose under Jan's cheek as he heaved a sigh. It held the sound of a peace hard won.

"Why don't you go call your folks and tell them we'll fly in tomorrow night? I'll drive over to the field this afternoon to make sure the plane's ready."

Jan withdrew from his arms reluctantly. "All right." She lifted a hand to wipe her cheeks, but Nick's warm fingers were there first. He smiled down at her crookedly.

"It'll be good to see Evan and Dolores again. You won't say anything?"

"No," Jan answered huskily.

He kissed her, his lips warm and loving. "My beautiful, gutsy little wife," he murmured as he pulled back. "I guess from now on we go by that corny motto: Live Each Day As If It Was Your Last."

"No." Jan shook her head firmly. "We'll live each day as if it was our *first*."

Their gazes locked, and she nearly started crying again when she saw the love and gratitude in his eyes.

"Yes," Nick said quietly. "I like that much better."

They went inside together, and Nick disappeared into his office while Jan placed the call to her mother. When she hung up, he was still wading through the mail. She wanted to go to him, be with him, but suspected he wanted some time alone. She went to the bedroom and packed a suitcase for each of them, then decided to see about fixing some lunch. They could eat out by the pool. Routine tasks were a blessing, she thought as she washed and sliced tomatoes, cucumbers, radishes and green onions for a salad; they kept both the mind and the body occupied. When she had everything ready, she carried a tray out to an umbrella-covered table at one side of the pool. She'd let Nick choose a wine. He enjoyed that, and he kept a good selection on hand.

Turning back toward the house to go tell him lunch was ready, she froze in her tracks. Her throat closed in fear. Her fingers and toes went cold, numb. He was standing on the top rung of a ladder propped against the rear of the house, near the corner, bent at the waist to stretch out over the tiled roof.

After a moment that first shock of alarm passed, and her pulse steadied and settled back to normal. She was being stupid, overreacting. How many times in the past three years had she seen him perched on top of a ladder or a chair or something equally precarious? She approached from his left, shading her eyes with one hand as she squinted up at him.

"Nick?" she called softly, not wanting to startle him. "What on earth are you doing?"

"I noticed the other day that a couple of these tiles were loose. Thought I'd better take care of them before we leave."

He backed down a rung on the ladder so that he could safely turn to look at her. For the rest of his life he would remember the picture she made at that moment: a bronzed goddess, bare-legged, her sleek black hair swinging free to her waist as she stood with her head tipped back.

"God, but you're beautiful."

"Thank you very much." Jan dropped a graceful curtsy. "Would you please get down from there? You're making me nervous. Besides, lunch is ready."

Nick grinned and started down. "Why didn't you say so right off, woman? I'm starved."

He'd reached the fourth rung from the bottom when a loud yelping at the front of the house made him temporarily halt his descent.

"What the devil...?"

"Sounds like Dawg," Jan answered with a frown. "He's probably out chasing rabbits or something."

"Well, I wish he'd find somewhere else to chase them. Lord, what a racket!"

His right foot reached for the next rung as he grumbled the complaint. At that instant a long-eared jackrabbit bounded around the corner of the house, with Dawg in hot pursuit.

"No!" Jan cried helplessly as both animals made straight for the base of the ladder. *"Nick!"*

His head jerked around and down as he stopped again. He felt a flash of blinding pain, and then Dawg hit the ladder, all eighty-five pounds of him, running full out. When Nick landed on the patio, he was already unconscious.

THREE HOURS LATER Jan stood facing a window in a visitors' lounge in the nearest hospital, which happened to possess one of the most up-to-date trauma-treatment centers in the country. Traffic streamed by on the wide avenue below, pedestrians hurried on their way, but she saw nothing, heard nothing, felt nothing. She was still wearing the faded cutoffs and T-shirt, though she did have sandals on her feet now, thanks to Allen.

He paced restlessly behind her. Every few seconds his reflection appeared in the window as he recrossed the room. He was chain-smoking, and his normally cheerful face was drawn and haggard with the strain of waiting.

He'd been out riding, exercising one of his horses with Dawg along for company. Jan's hysterical screams brought him around the house and onto the patio at a gallop, but of course by then it was too late.

She had tried to explain that to him through her grief as she knelt beside Nick, clutching at his hand and wetting his face with her tears, but Allen wouldn't listen. He checked for a pulse and respiration, then dashed into the house. Twenty minutes later Jan and Nick were on a LifeFlight helicopter en route to the hospital, Allen following in the Mustang.

When a hand gently came to rest on her shoulder, Jan stiffened. The moment she had been waiting for had come. They had sent someone to tell her that her husband was dead. Or dying. She'd thought she was prepared, but as a wave of bitter anguish swept through her she realized she would never be prepared, no matter how much time she had. Her facial muscles were stiff with the effort of control as she turned from the window. There was a nurse at Allen's side.

"She says the doctor wants to see you," he said, his voice rough. He, too, expected the worst.

"Come with me," Jan asked, and he nodded and grasped her hand in a tight grip.

They were led down a corridor, to a door marked Radiology. Jan frowned; it wasn't where she'd expected to be taken. Inside a tiny office a slender man in a white lab coat waited. He rose and gestured for them to take a couple of chairs on the other side of his desk.

"Mrs. Alexander, I'm Dr. Ian MacDonald." His soft Scottish burr was a surprise. "I asked you to come here because I want you to understand your husband's condition as completely as possible, and for that you need to see his X rays."

"I...I don't understand," Jan got out in a feeble whisper. "The shell fragment...when he fell, didn't it—"

"No, it did not sever his spinal cord," the doctor interrupted emphatically. "In fact, from what I've been able to tell from the films we took in Emergency, there's a good chance it didn't even come in contact."

Jan sat up straight on the hard-backed chair. Her eyes misted over, her hands clenched in her lap, and then she fainted dead away.

When she came to, she was lying on a cheap sofa covered in olive-green vinyl. Allen and Dr. MacDonald were both standing over her. Allen looked concerned. The doctor didn't, particularly. She sat up and swung her feet to the floor.

"Are you okay, Jan?" Allen asked anxiously.

"Yes, fine. I'm sorry. It was just the shock." She still had trouble accepting what she'd heard. She gazed up at the doctor, her eyes seeking confirmation.

He smiled kindly, then pulled one of the chairs over to sit facing her, eye to eye. She liked that.

"You were expecting bad news. I should have realized that when you mentioned the shell fragment. I apologize for my lack of diplomacy," he said. "I recognized your husband's name, of course. I assume this piece of shrapnel is a souvenir from his years as a war correspondent?"

Jan nodded, then explained everything to him, omitting nothing. She was aware of Allen's stunned expression as he listened, and could guess at what he was thinking: he was probably blaming himself, as Dawg's owner. Jan knew that wasn't right, but at the moment she couldn't be distracted long enough to console or reassure him. The only thing that mattered was finding out what Nick's current condition was, and his prognosis for the future. She asked Dr. MacDonald point-blank.

"That is precisely why I wanted you to see these, Mrs. Alexander," he said as he rose to his feet. He went to switch on a light behind a row of X rays clipped to the wall.

An hour later she still didn't have a definite answer. There were too many variables, as Dr. MacDonald had put it in his pleasantly accented voice. It was all far too complicated for Jan to comprehend right away, but she knew she was expected to make a decision, and quickly, whether she felt prepared or not. She closed her eyes and hugged her arms across her chest. Oh, God, what should she do? She'd never felt more alone in her life, and the one person who could have helped her lay unconscious in a room three floors below her, his life apparently in the balance.

"Tell me if I've got this straight, doctor," Allen said quietly. Jan looked up in surprise. He'd sat through the entire explanation without commenting, though she imagined he understood far more of it than she did. After all, he was a doctor, too; and the central nervous system of humans wasn't all that different from that of other mammals.

"You're saying that most likely the fall actually saved Nick's life, in that the fragment in the cervical area had entered the critical zone, but was deflected at the last minute, when he hit the patio?"

Dr. MacDonald nodded firmly. "That would seem to be the case, from these X rays," he agreed. "Of course, it's impossible to diagnose the exact extent of the trauma without actually exposing the fragment and the surrounding tissue."

"Yes, of course. I think Jan understands that, don't you, honey?"

She nodded, her face pale and strained. "Yes. I understand why it's necessary for Dr. MacDonald to operate there, at Nick's neck, to get at the piece of shrapnel. But this other problem I'm not sure I—"

"Okay, we'll cover that next." Allen's confident voice cut across her poorly articulated question and Jan sat back, glad to have him clarify things as much as he could. He glanced at the other man. "I'll explain it as well as I can, and if I make a mistake Dr. MacDonald can correct me." The surgeon nodded without speaking, and he went on.

"When Nick fell, he landed on his back, but not flat out. Maybe it was because of the pain from his neck, or maybe he was trying to turn and jump clear—whatever the reason, his spine was twisted at an unnatural angle when he hit. The fall itself caused small, hairline fractures in two of his vertebrae. You can see them on the X rays. The thing is, it looks like the *other* shell fragment somehow got dislodged, too, and now it's creating a whole new problem. It's just

one of those freak things that it happened to come to
rest at exactly the point where his spine's already
weakened by the fractures. It has to come out, Jan,
now. It's very unstable. Anything could cause it to
shift again, even moving him to change a dressing.
Do you understand what I'm saying?''

"Could he die from this?'' she whispered in
dread. "Are you telling me that the metal in his neck
didn't kill him—*won't* kill him—but that this other
piece could?'' Her voice and her eyes implored him
to reassure her that, no, there was no chance of that
happening if she refused to give the go-ahead for the
surgery Dr. MacDonald wanted to perform. Dear
God, she needed more time!

Allen's eyes were filled with compassion as he
took her hand in his. "I'm afraid it's possible, Jan.
He could start to hemorrhage or develop any number of life-threatening complications. Not to mention the certainty of at least partial paralysis if the
fragment should manage to reach the spinal cord.''

"But that's a possibility, anyway, even *with* the
surgery, isn't it?'' she challenged, turning to Dr.
MacDonald.

"Yes, it is a possibility,'' he answered at once.
"How great a possibility, I can't predict, until I get in
there and see what damage has already been done.''

Jan shook her head vehemently. "That's not good
enough, doctor. You'll have to do better than that.
Give me some percentages, some odds... something
to go on, for heaven's sake!''

His sandy brows drew together over the bridge of
his nose in a deep frown, and then he turned away.
He went to stand in front of the row of X rays and
stayed there a long time. When he finally turned
back to face her, Jan felt she'd lived an entire lifetime—all of it in purgatory.

"I don't like to give odds, Mrs. Alexander," he said slowly, carefully. "I'm a surgeon, not a bookmaker. But in this case...I feel guardedly optimistic about your husband's chances of coming through surgery with few or no complications. I'd say his odds for a full and complete recovery are better than fifty-fifty, and that's as far as I'm prepared to go."

Better than fifty-fifty. Jan closed her eyes again, stifling a hysterical laugh. She had her answer, and it didn't change a thing. The decision was still hers to make, and God help her—God help Nick—if she made the wrong one.

She opened her eyes and squared her shoulders. There was really only one thing she could do, after all. She'd known it for the past hour. All this business about needing more information, wanting things explained more fully, had just been a means of stalling for time. But now her time had run out. She lifted her chin and looked into the surgeon's kind brown eyes.

"Give me the forms and tell me where to sign," she said calmly.

6

THE REST OF THAT DAY and a good part of the night were spent waiting. Waiting and praying. Dr. MacDonald was heading the surgical team, which reassured Jan tremendously; still, nothing could completely allay her anxiety or ease the tension as the hours dragged by.

It was almost two in the morning when the exhausted surgeon shuffled through the lounge door. He was still in his surgical greens. He reached up to tug off his cap, leaving his wispy hair standing on end. Jan and Allen rose slowly to their feet. They were reluctant, half-afraid to ask what they were desperate to know. They gravitated toward each other and met in front of the weary surgeon, impulsively reaching out to clasp hands.

"Both operations were successful," Dr. MacDonald said, not making them wait a minute more than they already had. "He came through in excellent condition. His vital signs are all strong, and I don't anticipate any problems other than the postsurgical trauma we normally expect to see. His system's had quite a shock—including two major operations—but I expect his recovery to proceed without serious complication."

Jan sagged against Allen as his arm came around her. "Thank God," she breathed fervently. "When can I see him?"

"Not for several hours, I'm afraid. He's in surgical

Intensive Care right now. That's standard procedure, but it means no visitors, not even wives," the doctor emphasized. "I suggest you find somewhere to catch a few hours' sleep and come back later this morning. I'll have more to tell you then."

A sudden chill enveloped Jan. "Dr. MacDonald, is he—will he be paralyzed?" she forced herself to ask.

He reached out to touch her arm in a comforting gesture, only Jan wasn't comforted. Especially not when he advised gently, "Let's leave the questions and the answers for later. As I said, I'll have more information then."

Allen, bless him, had had the foresight to stick her suitcase in the Mustang before he left the house, so when he found a motel nearby she was able to shower and put on a gown and a robe. He insisted they both eat something, and went out for roast-beef sandwiches, French fries and coffee.

"If he is paralyzed, he's going to blame me," Jan said with quiet conviction as she picked at the food.

Allen sat back and gave her a penetrating look. "Because he'd already made up his mind that death would be preferable to living with a disability?" He crumpled his sandwich wrapper and lobbed it into the wastepaper basket in the corner as if he was delivering a grenade to an enemy bunker. "That's just plain crazy!"

Jan's smile was strained. "Not to Nick it isn't." She stabbed at a puddle of ketchup with a limp French fry. "I think he's more afraid of being helpless, dependent on other people, than he is of dying. He grew up in an orphanage, did you know that?"

"No," Allen said quietly. "You think that's got something to do with his attitude?"

Jan leaned back in the molded plastic chair, sighing wearily. "I think it probably does. Being on your own from childhood would have to affect your attitude about independence, wouldn't it? Then, too, he's seen some really horrible things in his life—first as an investigative reporter, and then in Vietnam. He always tried to be objective, not to let his personal feelings come through in his reporting, but I could tell when a story had really gotten to him. Usually it was the children or the old people—the two most helpless segments of any society."

"But, Jan, it would be totally unfair to blame you, whatever the outcome. You had no choice."

"Oh, but I did," she contradicted softly. "I could have respected his wishes, stood back and let him die."

"You couldn't have done that, honey. I know that, and Nick must, too. Everything will be fine, you'll see."

Jan didn't reply, though she had grave doubts. And she noticed that Allen didn't reassure her that her fears were probably groundless, that when she spoke to Dr. MacDonald, he would assure her that Nick's recovery would be full and complete.

Allen didn't expect a miracle any more than she did.

Before returning to the hospital, Jan phoned her parents to let them know she and Nick wouldn't be arriving that night as planned, and why. They were both shocked and concerned, of course, but warmly supportive, as she'd known they would be. She promised to let them know more after she'd spoken to the doctor and seen Nick.

Dr. MacDonald looked rested and refreshed, though he couldn't have gotten any more sleep than she had. He saw her in a different office this time, just down the hall from the surgical ICU. Allen chose to stay in the lounge, despite her assurances that he was welcome to come along.

"I have more good news," Dr. MacDonald said when Jan was seated across the desk from him. "He had an uneventful night and came out of the anesthetic about thirty minutes ago, though he'll be drifting in and out for a while yet. We've upgraded his condition from serious to fair, and I expect to move him from the ICU this afternoon."

Jan was thrilled, but surprised. "So soon?"

The surgeon's smile was meant to reassure her, and it did. "It's true that normally I wouldn't consider removing a patient from the ICU after this type of surgery quite this soon. But your husband is not the typical patient, I'm happy to say. His recuperative powers have amazed the entire staff. When I changed his dressings this morning, the surgical wounds looked like those of a patient in his third or fourth day of recovery. At the rate he's progressing, I wouldn't be surprised if he's ready for discharge well ahead of schedule. Of course, all this presupposes that the internal healing proceeds as rapidly as the external."

"Which brings us to the question of the hour, doesn't it?" Jan said solemnly. "You put me off last night, Dr. MacDonald, but I won't be put off forever. I want to know if there's any paralysis, and if there is, how extensive is it?"

"It's a little early to tell," he answered, then held up a hand when she would have objected. "No, wait, I'm not putting you off, Mrs. Alexander. For one thing, your husband is not yet fully alert, as I explained before. Until he is, all we can do is check for involuntary reflexive response, and even that won't be conclusive for a while yet."

"Why not?" Jan demanded softly.

He leaned back in his chair, tapping the edge of his desk with a pencil as he explained, apparently not at all upset by her perseverance.

"I was correct in believing the shell fragment in the cervical area hadn't damaged the cord itself, which is very good, as I'm sure you realize." Jan nodded, but didn't comment, and he went on. "However, there was some mild trauma, enough to cause what we refer to as cord shock. That means that for an indeterminate period—probably no more than thirty-six hours, at a guess—the effect will be the same as if the cord *had* been damaged. Am I making the situation clear?"

"Yes, I believe so," Jan said cautiously. "So that's why testing his reflexes won't be conclusive, at least until this cord shock wears off."

"Exactly. As for the other injury," he continued, sitting forward and clasping his hands on the desk blotter, "it may be some time before we know for sure whether there'll be any permanent paralysis. I was able to remove the second piece of shrapnel without much difficulty. It didn't appear to have done any serious damage, either, but there are still the two fractures to consider."

He paused, pursing his lips in thoughtful consideration, and Jan waited, tense and silent, not daring to interrupt or ask any more questions.

"I *think*—" the soft emphasis he gave the word wasn't wasted on her "—that at this point things look good. Extremely encouraging. If I had to make a prognosis today, based on the success of the surgery and this morning's examination . . . ."

In the silence during his next pause Jan could hear her pulse drumming in her ears, feel it hammering at her temples.

"I would predict that your husband could possibly be on his feet again in...oh, let's give it six months, just to be on the safe side."

He suddenly sat bolt upright in his chair, frowning at her across the desk.

"Mrs. Alexander! You're not going to faint on me again, are you?"

"No," Jan whispered, then repeated it with more conviction. "No, I'm not going to faint. I may kiss you, though," she said with a blinding smile.

Dr. MacDonald grinned boyishly. "If you still feel the urge in six months, Mrs. Alexander, I certainly won't beat you off with a stick."

Her smile slipped a little. "*If* I still feel the urge?"

"If," he confirmed softly. "Six months can be a very long time, Mrs. Alexander."

Jan was too happy—euphoric would have been a better word—to let his cautionary words or the vaguely troubled look in his eyes make any lasting impression. Nick was going to be all right! She hurried to the lounge to share the news with Allen, then phoned her mother, who promised to call her father at the paper right away and then stated her intention to fly out that night.

"Oh, mom, I appreciate the thought, but it's not necessary, really."

"Don't argue with your mother, Janet Faye. I'll rent a car at the airport and go straight to that motel you called from before. You'd better give me the name and address." When she'd copied the information and repeated it, she added quietly, "Nick is like a son to us, you know. Where should a mother be when her children have trouble? I'll see you sometime tonight, dear. Give Nick our love when you see him."

Knowing that Allen had stock to see to and patients to treat, Jan sent him home. Since her mother

would have a rental car, he was free to take Nick's
Mustang. He made her promise to phone him with
regular reports when he kissed her goodbye in the
ground-floor lobby. She had lunch in the hospital
coffee shop and then went back upstairs to wait until Nick was moved to a private room and she could
see him. It was almost three o'clock when Dr. Mac-
Donald sought her out to tell her the room transfer
had been made.

"But I want a word with you first," he said as he
took her arm and led her to a sofa in one corner of
the lounge.

"What is it? Has something gone wrong?" Jan
asked anxiously.

"No, no, nothing's gone wrong," he hastened to
assure her. "At least, not physically. It's his mental
state, or perhaps I should say his emotional state, I
want to talk to you about."

"Prepare me for, you mean," Jan said quietly.

The surgeon gazed into her solemn eyes and nodded. "Yes. Prepare you for."

"What's happened? No, I can guess. When he became fully conscious, alert, he was still suffering the
effects of this cord shock you told me about."

"Precisely. To make matters worse, I was in emergency surgery and couldn't get up to see him for
about two hours."

"Oh, no," Jan whispered, closing her eyes. *Nick.
Oh, my love, my poor darling love.* Two hours of lying
there helplessly, thinking his worst nightmare had
come true.

"When I did see him I explained, of course, but
I'm afraid that by then the damage had been done."
Dr. MacDonald paused, gazing at her intently, gain-
ing her full attention. "Mrs. Alexander, he doesn't
believe that this is only a temporary condition. He's

convinced the paralysis he's experiencing now is permanent, and he's very—"

"Bitter," Jan supplied in a flat, emotionless voice. "He's bitter, and he's angry." Her stoic calm obviously surprised him. "Thank you for warning me, Dr. MacDonald." She stood, and he rose with her. "I'd like to see him now."

"I don't want you to be alarmed when you go in," the surgeon told her as they walked down the corridor. "Because of the surgery and the fractures, we've had to immobilize him."

Jan shot him a mocking glance. "I'd have thought the paralysis would have seen to that."

"Not effectively, I'm afraid," he answered in his quiet, unperturbed voice. "For one thing, there'll be muscle spasms to contend with, and for another a patient can't be left in the same position for an extended period of time."

Jan nodded. "Pressure sores," she said succinctly.

"Yes. Fortunately medical science has come up with an effective, though I'll grant not particularly comfortable or pleasant-looking, solution. You've probably seen these things on television," he remarked as he stood aside at the door of a private room to let her enter first. "It's rather ingenious, actually."

Ingenious wasn't a word Jan would have chosen to describe the tubular contraption surrounding her husband. Her first reaction was that it looked like some modern-day instrument of torture. The outer frame resembled a Ferris wheel, only instead of seats there was a sort of stretcher slung across the diameter, and on it, strapped down in half a dozen places, lay Nick.

Her dismay must have shown, because Dr. Mac-Donald laid a hand on her arm and frowned at her severely before backing out of the room to leave the two of them alone.

At the moment, the only active part of Nick's body was his mind, which was writhing in agony as he stared down at the perfectly aligned tiles on the floor. He registered the muted *whoosh* of the pneumatically controlled door as it closed, but couldn't even turn his head to see who had entered the room. Then came the rhythmic *tap, tap* of a woman's heels. Not a nurse; their shoes were either silent or squeaked. It had to be Jan, then. He mentally recoiled at having her see him like this. Though he could only imagine the sight he made, he'd visited enough V.A. hospitals for the image to be cruelly accurate. He had no trouble visualizing the restraints binding him to the stretcher frame, the needles, the tubes, the repellent catheter bag, his own helpless body....

No! Dear God, no! Go away! Don't look at me!

He stopped breathing for a moment as panic clawed at his throat. Had he vocalized the plea, or had it stayed inside his skull? His pride was a terrible liability at that moment. He needed to be comforted more than he'd ever needed anything in his life; yet pride demanded that he retain as much dignity as he could. He might be trapped in a ruined, useless body, but inside that body the heart of a man still beat; the pride of a man still required an effort at composure, control.

Her shoes entered the limited scope of his vision, and the trimness of her ankles and the shapely curve of her calves gave him both pleasure and pain. He didn't speak. He couldn't trust himself to.

"Nick?" she said softly. "Are you awake?"

He didn't answer. She sank to her knees, then found she still wasn't low enough and sat down on the floor, supporting herself with one arm as she leaned sideways to see his face. His eyes were open, but he wouldn't look at her. He just kept staring fixedly at the floor.

"Nick? Darling, are you in pain?"

The anxious concern in her voice was intolerable. Hell, yes, he was in pain, but it was more mental than physical, and it was caused by her betrayal.

"What have you done to me, Jan?" His harsh voice sounded guttural to his own ears, because of the sling under his jaw. "Damn it, what have you done to me?" His voice hoarsened and actually broke on the last two words.

She didn't immediately respond, but he could feel her watching him. He didn't attempt to say anything more, letting his silence serve as accusation.

"Nick," Jan finally murmured, her voice carefully controlled, "Dr. MacDonald told me he'd spoken to you, explained—"

"To hell with Dr. MacDonald!" The words spewed out of him in a savage snarl. "Nobody could have opened me up, cut into my body, if you hadn't agreed. You knew, dammit! You *knew!*" It was a tortured cry, torn from the depths of his soul. "I thought I could trust you!"

Jan closed her eyes tight and let the words flay her, forcing herself not to curl up in a whimpering ball.

"Nick, will you listen, please?" she begged quietly. "The situation had changed. When you fell off the ladder, the piece of metal in your neck was deflected. It shifted away from the spinal cord. *Away*, do you understand! It wasn't the way those other doctors predicted it would be. This paralysis you're experiencing is only temporary. Dr. MacDonald told you that and you have to believe him, because it's true! I swear, Nick, it's true!" she repeated on a note of desperation.

"I'm no fool, Jan," he said in a flat voice. "I know how doctors soft-pedal the bad news, doling it out slowly in the beginning until they figure the patient's strong enough to hear the whole rotten truth. Well, I already know. I knew when I woke up and couldn't feel a damned thing from the neck down." His mouth twisted in a bitter grimace. "When I married you, I thought I was buying insurance against this very eventuality. Ironic, isn't it? At least with Marina, I'd have known what to expect."

"Nick, don't," Jan pleaded tearfully. "If you'll just be patient, you'll see—"

"Patient!" he repeated viciously. "Be patient, she says, as if I've got any choice." His eyes suddenly closed, and a spasm contorted his face. "I'm tired, and my neck hurts like hell. Do me a favor and get out of here, will you—just go away and leave me alone. On the way out, see if you can find somebody to give me something to knock me out," he added hoarsely. "Then at least I won't have to lie here and think about my beautiful young wife and how she's betrayed my trust."

Jan made it into the corridor, then sagged against the wall in despair. Dr. MacDonald was waiting. He didn't speak, giving her time to compose herself, and Jan was grateful.

"He's in pain," she eventually said. "From his neck. Could you please give him something?"

He stopped a passing nurse and asked her to bring Mr. Alexander's chart. When she had, he wrote an order for medication on it. The nurse read it, nodded and hurried off to carry out her instructions.

"That should give him relief without actually putting him under. I don't want him leaving here a junkie." When Jan didn't react to the wry comment, he peered at her strained features closely. "Are you all right, Mrs. Alexander? Would you like to lie down for a while? You're welcome to use my office."

She shook her head and straightened from the wall. "No, thank you. It was just worse than I'd anticipated, that's all. I'll be fine."

"I never doubted it," he said with a grave smile. "You're an exceptionally strong woman, Mrs. Alexander. I expect both you and your husband will rely on that strength rather heavily in the weeks and months ahead."

Jan sank back against the wall, closing her eyes in exhaustion. "If what happened in there just now is any indication, doctor, my husband requires nothing more of me than my absence."

"Why don't you go back to your motel?" he suggested gently. "Things will surely look better tomorrow morning. I can prescribe something to help you sleep tonight, if you like."

Jan thanked him for the offer, but refused. She walked the short distance to the motel, and then wished she hadn't come straight back. The rest of the afternoon and evening stretched before her like a bleak expanse of desert.

As it turned out, she didn't have to spend all those long, empty hours alone, though. Shortly after seven there was a knock on the door. Wondering who on earth it could be, Jan answered it to find her mother standing outside with two pieces of matched luggage on the ground beside her.

"Mother! How on earth...?"

"I was lucky enough to catch an early flight. Carry one of these in for me, will you, dear?" she requested calmly as she hefted a suitcase and stepped past Jan into the room. "Frankly, I'm bushed."

When the luggage had been deposited beside one of the twin beds, they embraced wordlessly. Then Dolores stood back and gave her daughter a quick but thorough once-over.

"I was surprised when the manager said you were in your room. I expected you to still be at the hospital. Talk to me, Janet Faye. Tell me about it."

Jan felt tears spurt to her eyes. Her lower lip started to tremble, and the next thing she knew both she and her mother were sitting on one of the beds and she was crying her heart out. When her sobs had abated, she got up and went into the tiny bathroom to wash her face, then returned and calmly told her mother the whole story.

Dolores St. Clair possessed many of the attributes of her ancestors, among them the capacity for maintaining her poise in times of crisis. She patted her daughter's hand in a comforting gesture, her dark eyes filled with compassion.

"Well, I expect the doctor's right. Things *will* look better in the morning. By then Nick will have realized he isn't permanently paralyzed, and you can both put the past couple of days behind you. I'll bet you've hardly eaten all day. Go put on some makeup to cover those puffy eyes, and I'll treat you to dinner."

"Oh, mother." Jan couldn't help laughing weakly. "You're a godsend. Give me ten minutes."

They went out to a small family-style restaurant a few blocks from the motel and caught up on each other's news when they returned. By the time they were ready for bed Jan felt hopeful, if not confident, that things would somehow work out for the best. Nick *would* forgive her for going against his wishes, once he realized his condition wasn't permanent, she assured herself, and steadfastly ignored the nagging, persistent doubt at the back of her mind.

"You look lovely," Dolores claimed as they prepared to leave for the hospital the following morning. "If seeing you doesn't lift my son-in-law's spirits, nothing will."

Jan glanced down at the peach suit she'd been married in. "I wanted to wear something cheerful. Unfortunately, just about all I have with me is jeans and T-shirts. We'd planned on a quiet weekend just visiting with you and daddy, and I packed accordingly. Nick's suitcase is still on the bed at home," she added huskily, biting on her lower lip to still its sudden quiver. "Oh, mom—"

"None of that now, Janet Faye!" Dolores admonished. "We agreed, remember? The tone for today is upbeat, positive. No moping, and positively no tears!"

"But I'm so afraid," Jan admitted shakily. "What if—"

"No 'what ifs,' either! I'm surprised at you, Janet St. Clair Alexander! You've never been one to quit when the going gets rough, and this is certainly no time to start."

"But, mother, this is different, don't you understand?"

"Of course I do. You're terrified that one way or another you might lose the man you love, the only man you've ever loved," Dolores said softly. She smiled at Jan's stunned expression. "Oh, Janet, did you honestly think we didn't know? My heart ached for you when he married that Calhoun woman. I still think he must have temporarily taken leave of his senses—she was never any good for him, and anybody with two eyes in his head could see it."

She placed her hands on Jan's shoulders and looked deep into her eyes. "But you *are* good for him, and don't you ever doubt it. He's yours now. He's committed himself to you, and you to him, for better or worse. If you let this rocky patch destroy your chance for happiness, you're no daughter of mine. Your father and I both believe in fighting for what we want out of life—tooth and nail, to the bitter end—and we tried to raise you to be the same way. Now grab your purse and let's go. Your husband's waiting, and he needs you, whether he realizes it or not. Remember that!"

Jan held fast to those words, clasping them to her heart, clinging to them. Nick needed her. She knew it was true, yet she also knew that she needed him every bit as much, perhaps more.

Dr. MacDonald had left word at the nurses' station that she was to go directly to Nick's room. Expecting the doctor to be there already, she started down the corridor. Dolores accompanied her as far as the entrance to the lounge and then stopped.

"Mother..." Jan began anxiously.

"Oh, no. You're not hiding behind me," Dolores said firmly. "You can come and get me later, after you've had your reunion. Go to your husband, Janet Faye, and for heaven's sake wipe that stricken look off your face! You look like you're on the way to a funeral."

Jan made a conscious effort to relax and had pretty well succeeded by the time she pulled open the door to Nick's room and stepped inside. It took about two seconds for her to tense up again when she registered the fact that Dr. MacDonald wasn't there.

She couldn't face Nick. Not yet...not until she'd first prepared herself by talking to the surgeon. She turned to leave, her arm extended to push the door open so she could slip out like the coward she was, before he even knew she was there.

"Jan? Is that you?"

She froze, torn between answering and fleeing. Her palm was already flat against the varnished wood. He couldn't see her, so he couldn't *know* it was she. All she had to do was push, then hope her unsteady legs could get her through the door and into the corridor.

"Jan? Don't leave, please."

It was as if he felt her indecision, the turmoil inside her. His voice was low and coaxing, almost pleading. It tore at her heart. She closed her eyes and made herself breathe deeply. Her hand was withdrawn from the door. *Please*, she prayed silently. Aloud, she said, "I thought you might be sleeping." She was dismayed to hear the cool, slightly aloof tone of her voice.

There was a brief pause before Nick responded. "No. I've been waiting for you." Another pause. This one felt a little hesitant, a little uncertain. "Will you come over here so I can see you?"

There was no way to refuse without betraying her tension and nervousness. Jan crossed the room toward the intimidating metal structure surrounding and supporting him, her legs so shaky she was afraid her knees might start knocking together. She stopped directly in front of him, her hands clenched on her purse. He looked so helpless strapped down like that. She wanted to fall down beside him and cradle his head in her arms and scatter loving kisses all over his face. Instead she stood rigidly, terrified of rejection if she made even the slightest sympathetic overture.

"How's your neck today?" she asked stiffly, wanting to know and yet half-afraid he'd snarl at her for asking.

"It still hurts like the devil, but I'm getting used to

it," Nick answered dryly. "Would you mind pulling a chair over here or something? I like those shoes, but I feel ridiculous talking to them."

They both knew that even if she sat in a chair he wouldn't be able to raise his eyes farther than her lap. Jan pressed her lips together for a moment, and then gracefully sank to the floor, her legs folded under her so that she could half recline, as she'd done the day before. She couldn't bring herself to look into his face, though, keeping her gaze focused on a point just beyond his right shoulder.

"That's the outfit you were married in."

The soft statement caught her unprepared for the thrill it sent through her. She hadn't expected him to remember.

"Yes," she answered in a whisper. She lifted her free hand, the one that wasn't supporting her, to tuck her hair behind an ear, then started to repeat the gesture on the other side of her face.

"Let me," Nick said huskily. And then his fingers, warm and infinitely gentle, were brushing her cheek, caressing the sleek fall of her hair as they lifted it and settled it behind her ear.

Jan's eyes closed as the blood drained from her face. Blindly, she reached up to capture his hand, turning her face to it, pressing her lips against his warm skin. She trembled in joyful relief, and slow tears leaked from beneath her lashes to wet his thumb. Nick's fingers closed around hers, his grip firm and sure.

"Nick, Nick," she whispered in a moist, broken voice. "Thank God. I was so afraid." She kissed his hand again—hard, fervent kisses that eased some of her anxiety and the fear that had gripped her since she left him the day before.

"Jan." His voice was shaken, too, and thick with

emotion. When she opened her eyes, she was shocked by the remorse and self-condemnation she saw in his.

"Forgive me," he asked hoarsely. "Oh, baby, forgive me. I was a bastard to you yesterday. I'm sorry. It's just that I was so—"

She moved their clasped hands, shushing him by placing the back of hers against his lips. And then the link was broken as she scooted closer to replace her hand with her mouth. Nick couldn't move his head, not even a centimeter, but she seemed to know exactly where he wanted her to kiss him, and how. Her lips flitted over his face, touching every square inch of it before returning to his mouth to linger sweetly, lovingly. She felt his hands touch her cheeks, slide into her hair with a trembling joy, then continue on to the back of her neck and shoulders. When their cheeks brushed in passing she wondered if the moisture she felt had all come from her eyes. It didn't matter. Only two things mattered at that moment: Nick was going to be all right, and he still loved her.

7

JAN BACKED AWAY A LITTLE, smiling radianty through her tears. She held her hands up at shoulder level, and Nick pressed his palms to hers, aligning their fingers perfectly. She laughed and leaned forward to kiss him again. He was ready. When her mouth opened over his, his tongue slipped inside with a tenderness that brought fresh tears to her eyes.

"I love you," he whispered against her lips. "I love you so much!" His voice was husky with emotion, and his fingers suddenly laced with hers to squeeze her hands. The strength of his grip was surprising. "I was so afraid I'd driven you away, that you wouldn't come back."

Jan withdrew just enough to shake her head. She gently rubbed her knuckles over his full lower lip. "When you fell off that ladder, you must have scrambled your brains," she said with a watery smile. "I love you, too, you dope."

Nick's eyes closed, but not before she saw the relief that filled them. "That's good to know," he murmured roughly.

She gave him a moment to compose himself, then said softly, "Mother's here. Do you feel up to seeing her for a few minutes?"

Nick's eyes flew open again. "Dolores? Here?"

"Mm-hmm. Right down the hall, in the visitors' lounge. She flew in last night."

"Then you weren't alone." There was a slight residual roughness to his voice. "I'm glad. I worried about you."

"I worried about you, too," Jan admitted softly. "And about us—whether you wanted there to be an us anymore."

Nick's grip tightened in remorse, the pressure of his fingers a physical extension of the emotion in his piercing green eyes. "There'll always be an us," he said hoarsely. "There has to be." His voice dropped to a throaty murmur, as if he didn't trust himself to speak any louder. "I do love you. Promise you'll remember that, no matter—"

Jan sensed his sudden anxiety. She returned his grip with equal force, her love shining from her eyes. "I'll remember. I may even remind you from time to time."

The remark coaxed a strained smile from him. "Feel free," he said quietly.

"Nick? Darling, what is it?"

For a moment his grip became painful. When he answered the control he was exerting made his voice sound flat. "The feeling's only come back to about the middle of my chest. Below that...nothing."

"Have you spoken to Dr. MacDonald about it?" Jan asked cautiously. She wasn't about to reassure him, raise his hopes, until she knew whether the surgeon's opinion had changed.

"Oh, yeah. Good ol' Dr. Mac was infuriatingly noncommittal. He says it's a little early to be a hundred percent sure, but this will probably turn out to be only temporary, too."

"Well, then." Jan's smile was genuine as the tension inside her eased. "That should reassure you."

"Should it?" Nick searched her face intently, as if looking for a sign, something that would contradict the optimistic conviction in her voice. "The two of you haven't entered into some well-meant conspiracy of silence, have you? If you knew something, you wouldn't keep it from me?''

Jan could feel the strain he was under as he waited for her answer. She squeezed his hands hard and looked straight into his eyes. ''I wouldn't, and I'm not,'' she said softly but firmly. ''As a matter of fact, he told me pretty much the same thing yesterday morning.''

''And you believe him?'' Nick pressed. ''Trust his opinion?''

''Absolutely. He's good, Nick, and he hasn't withheld anything from me. Don't be afraid to believe him, darling. He won't lie to you, or tell you half truths.''

''Okay, if you say so,'' he sighed, exhaustion suddenly dulling his voice. ''I'll just have to tough it out a little longer.''

Jan rose to her knees and gently eased his arms back around the metal frame, arranging them to lie alongside him. ''You're tired,'' she murmured tenderly. ''You should rest awhile, get some sleep.'' She stroked his face lovingly. ''Do you need anything — are you having much pain?''

''No. I think you're right — I just need to rest.'' His eyes started to drift closed, then struggled open again. ''I forgot,'' he mumbled. ''Dolores.''

''Hush, darling. She'll still be here when you wake up. We'll both be here,'' Jan soothed. She kissed his temple, then very lightly pressed her cheek to his, conscious that she mustn't cause his head to move. She heard the way his shallow breath caught in his throat, and felt a muscle in his cheek twitch.

''Jan,'' he whispered hesitantly. ''I'm scared.''

A fierce, protective love filled her heart, overflowing to push up into her throat, nearly choking her.

She knew what the admission had cost his pride, how he would hate having her see his vulnerability, know of his fear. That he'd actually said the words told her how deep the emotion went, how acutely he felt it. Somehow she managed to keep her voice steady, though she couldn't do a thing about the tears that flooded her eyes.

"It's all right, darling. It's all right to be afraid," she murmured close to his ear.

"What if he's wrong? What if—"

"Shh, don't. He isn't wrong. Have faith." She interspersed the reassurances with soft kisses on his eyes and cheeks, longing to do more but knowing she mustn't.

She kissed him again as hard as she dared, deliberately forcing his thoughts in another direction. After a moment Nick sighed, his breath mingling sweetly with hers, but she waited another few seconds before she eased away. His eyes remained closed, and a relaxed smile tugged at one corner of his mouth. Jan moved her head to lightly touch her tongue to the spot, and he sighed again.

"Stay with me until I fall asleep," he asked drowsily.

"Wild horses couldn't drag me away."

"I need you." The words were spoken in so soft a whisper that Jan barely heard them. She swallowed hard, then brushed her lips across his temple.

"I'm here. I'll always be here. I need you, too."

Nick awoke slowly, in stages. First came the passive, contented drift into semiwakefulness; then the reluctant awareness that things were not exactly as they should be; and finally—as the persistent, throbbing pain made itself felt—full comprehension.

Despair came to roost between his shoulder blades,

the grip of its talons intensifying the pain until he wanted to howl. He fumbled for the box near his head and smashed his thumb down on the call button. In less than a minute a nurse arrived with a syringe. As the medication began to take effect he reflected that he must be pretty high on their priority list to rate such fast service. He wondered if he should be encouraged by that fact or worried.

He told himself he was getting paranoid, that he had to keep things in perspective. Both the surgeon and Jan had assured him this lousy situation was only temporary, and Jan wouldn't lie to him about something that important. The doctor, maybe, but not Jan.

He squeezed his eyes shut as he recalled the way he'd nearly broken down in front of her. Humiliation burned like a brand on his soul. Lord knew he'd never felt weaker, but he should have had more pride than to let his control slip like that, more self-respect. His worst dread was that she would pity him; yet he had all but begged for pity by letting her see how insecure and vulnerable he felt.

Never again, he vowed grimly. No matter how demoralized or depressed he became in the days and weeks ahead, Jan wouldn't know. Her love was too new, too fragile. It might not survive in a contest with pity; and if he lost her love now, he was damned sure *he* wouldn't survive.

IN THE FOLLOWING WEEKS Nick's resolve was sorely tested as the days dragged by and boredom alternated with frustration. So subtly that he sometimes doubted his own perception, sensation began to return; but gradually, and often as only an elusive tingling at first. Half the time he was afraid to believe it wasn't just wishful thinking. While he had made a conscious decision to accept the surgeon's prognosis, a deeply buried but powerful part of his subconscious was convinced that the doctor was only telling him what he wanted to hear, that the most he could expect was a lifetime sentence of being confined to a wheelchair.

Of course he never voiced this belief. He wasn't even aware of it himself most of the time. Only at the end of a particularly bad day, when no progress had been detected and his confidence was at low ebb, did he entertain such negative thoughts. The rest of the time he maintained a positive attitude, partly for his own peace of mind and partly to keep Jan happy.

Both she and Dolores were unfailingly optimistic, never once implying they harbored any misgivings about his recovery. In the face of their constant cheerful enthusiasm and encouragement, he couldn't find it in himself to express the doubts that had taken root in the darkest recesses of his mind.

After two weeks Dolores returned home, but Jan resolutely carried on the campaign they had begun together, her twin objectives to bolster Nick's spirits and prevent him from succumbing to depression. Dr. MacDonald—or Mac, as they had both started calling him—was her chief accomplice and ally. The diminutive Scot started regular physiotherapy sessions while Nick was still almost totally immobilized; and just as the novelty of that began to pall, he put his patient in a neck-to-hip brace and moved him from the Stryker frame to a regular hospital bed.

The weekend after Dolores left, Allen and Lisa came for a visit. Lisa drove her own car, and Allen brought Nick's Mustang to leave with Jan. On a brief trip home a few days later Jan discovered that the page proofs for *Fowler's Rage*, Nick's latest book, had arrived. She loaded them, along with a stack of his mail, into his briefcase and took everything to him in the hospital. Mac provided a slant board that could be placed over Nick's lap while he partially reclined in bed, and Jan put him to work. Answering letters and checking the proofs for errors took the better part of a week, during which he had neither time nor concentration to spare for boredom or frustration.

One afternoon during Nick's sixth week of hospitalization, Dr. MacDonald sought Jan out and asked her to come to his office. Nick was having a therapy session and wouldn't return to his room for another half hour. As soon as they were both seated, the surgeon proceeded in his usual straightforward style.

"He'll be ready for release in another week, give or take a couple of days."

Jan beamed at him, ecstatic at the news. "Mac, do you mean it? That's wonderful!" Then a thought occurred to her, and she sobered a little. "But he still hasn't regained sensation or function below the waist. How can he go home?"

The surgeon folded his slender hands on top of the desk, his expression solemn. "He'll go home the same way as most of the other patients from this floor—in a wheelchair, which he'll have to continue to use for several more weeks, at least."

After a short, thoughtful silence, Jan asked quietly, "Does he know? And more important, has he accepted it?"

"He knows I plan to release him within a week or so, and I have tried to discuss the problems he'll face, especially at first. But—" he spread his hands, palms up "—frankly, he doesn't want to hear. It's a fairly typical reaction. I've yet to meet a patient who welcomes having his limitations cataloged, and if he hasn't yet fully come to terms with them, himself—"

"Mac," Jan interrupted a little impatiently, "he's been here nearly six weeks. He can't help but be aware of his limitations. If anything, he's too aware of them."

"Exactly. And when he leaves here, the problems he already faces will only increase."

"Mac, that's ridiculous," Jan scoffed. "He'll be going *home*!"

"Yes," the surgeon murmured with a nod. "But while that home hasn't changed, he has." He made a sweeping gesture with one hand. "Here, everything accommodates the patients and their needs, *everything*, from the light switches to the toilet facilities. Except for restricted areas he's had access to any area of this wing, because the building was designed to be accessible to those whose physical mobility has been impaired. The purpose of getting him into a wheelchair as soon as possible was to help him regain his sense of independence, self-sufficiency, and it's worked. But I seriously doubt that your home is as suited to his present needs as this hospital, and once he's there even the simplest tasks may become exercises in futility and frustration. Of course, it doesn't have to be that way," he continued on a more encouraging note. "With the right attitude, and some preparation on your part, he can approach those same tasks as temporary obstacles to overcome or work around."

Jan nodded soberly. She was remembering the conversation she and Allen had had the night of Nick's surgery. He feared the prospect of being helpless and dependent even more than he feared the thought of death, she'd said then, and she still believed it was true.

"Exactly what kind of preparations can I make?" she asked. "Tell me what to do, Mac, and I'll do it."

"There are several excellent books I can recommend, primarily self-help guides for people with physical disabilities. Nick's therapist will be happy to advise you, as well. If you like, I'll make an appointment for you to talk with him."

"Fine," Jan agreed. "The sooner the better."

The following afternoon she informed Nick that she was going home that evening. He wasn't crazy about the idea of her making the trip after dark. He suggested she wait until the next day.

She smiled as she placed her hands on the arm-rests of his wheelchair and bent down to give him a light kiss. "If I wait till tomorrow, I'll miss a whole day with you," she pointed out. "But if I go tonight I can be back in time for us to have lunch together. Promise to be a good boy and not flirt with any of the nurses while I'm gone, and I'll sneak you in a Big Mac."

Nick frowned at her. "You drive a hard bargain, lady."

"You ain't seen nothin' yet," she promised with a suggestive grin. "Just wait'll I get you home, where I won't have to worry about one of your ministering angels barging in at an inopportune moment."

Nick's only response was to shake his head in mock reproof. He could hardly tell her that in some ways he'd been thankful for the lack of privacy during the past six weeks. He hated admitting it even to himself.

For the rest of the afternoon and until she left at eight, he gave an excellent impression of a man with nothing more on his mind than enjoying his wife's company. He smiled a lot, held Jan's hand as she sat beside him in his room, even suggested they go down to the lounge for a while, where they ended up playing cards with a couple of the other patients they'd gotten to know. When they returned to his room Jan went straight to the bed to turn back the blanket and top sheet, then stepped out of her shoes.

"Well?" she prompted when Nick halted his chair at the foot of the bed. "Come on, time to hit the sack."

"I'm not tired," he said, his voice oddly subdued. "It's only seven-thirty. I won't be sleepy for hours."

"Who said anything about sleeping?" Jan countered with a grin. She patted the mattress in invitation, not noticing the way his grip had tightened on the hand rims of the chair's wheels. "We've got time for a cuddle before I leave, and there's no better place for a cuddle than in bed. Come on, Alexander, don't give me a hard time. You can get up again after I'm gone, if you want."

She stepped away a little, making room for him to back the chair in next to the bed, and Nick acquiesced without further argument. He allowed Jan to help him remove his robe, but when he had grasped the trapeze hanging above the bed with one hand and was prepared to transfer from the chair, she bent toward him, clearly intending to take hold of his legs, and he protested.

"It's okay, I can manage."

"I know you can, but tonight you don't have to." Sliding her hands under his thighs, just above the knees, she looked up with a smile. "Just consider it one of my little wifely duties."

It had been a really dumb thing to say, she realized at once. Nick's mouth tightened in reaction and his back seemed to stiffen. She could have kicked herself as he turned his head toward the trapeze.

"You know I'm supposed to do as much as I can without help," he said as he firmed his grip on the bar and began to pull himself onto the mattress.

"That's the point of all the therapy, isn't it—to make me as independent as possible?" There was just a trace of sarcasm in his voice.

"And build up your strength again," Jan answered calmly as she shifted her hands to his ankles to lift and straighten his legs. "Yes, I do know." She impulsively leaned down to kiss him lightly but firmly on the mouth, then slipped onto the bed with him, stretching out full-length and nestling against his side. "I wasn't trying to sabotage your independence," she murmured as she laid her head on his shoulder and draped an arm across his chest. "And I apologize for the stupid remark about wifely duties, although I didn't mean it the way you obviously took it."

Nick's jerk of surprise was quickly controlled, but not before she felt it. She tipped her head back and found him staring down at her, his features once more relaxed and amusement glimmering in his eyes.

"Witch," he said softly. "Read me like a book, don't you?" He shoved an arm under her and cupped his hand to fit her hip. "I apologize, too," he sighed. "I guess I get a little defensive sometimes, huh?"

"You could say that," Jan agreed easily. "Sometimes you're as prickly as a porcupine, not to mention pigheaded and—"

"All right, all right, I never claimed to be perfect!"

"You are, though," she told him as she gazed into the warm green eyes so close to her own. "Perfect for me. Kiss me."

She didn't give him a chance to refuse the request, sliding her right shoulder over his left as she homed in on his mouth. The hand that had been resting on his rib cage drifted upward, over his shoulder to his

neck and then on to his head. She slipped her fingers
into his hair, lightly scraping his scalp with her nails
before she began to gently massage. Her other arm
was braced under her to hold her weight off him,
until Nick reached up to clasp her elbow and pull it
away. His fingers were warm on her skin as he
guided her arm up over his shoulder.

"I won't break," he murmured into her mouth.
He released her elbow to wrap his arm around her
and shift her further onto his chest.

"But..." Jan began uncertainly, and his free hand
suddenly clamped on the back of her head.

"No buts," he said firmly. He applied steady pressure to bring her head down, until her lips hovered
just above his. "You asked me to kiss you, remember? I'm only trying to oblige. Relax. I don't hurt
anywhere. If I do, I'll let you know."

As he pressed her head down that last millimeter,
her arms twined around his neck and she subsided
against him, the muscles of her shoulders going
slack. But she was still holding back, he could tell,
and it both irritated and frustrated him.

During the past couple of weeks he'd often wanted to tell her not to be so hesitant, that she wouldn't
injure him or cause him pain if she threw her arms
around him and hugged him or plopped down on
his lap so that he could hug her. He might not be
ready to enter any decathlons, but he was in pretty
good shape, all things considered.

Then, too, he was aware of a disturbing ambiva-
lence within himself. He wanted—*needed*—her to
touch him, to know she still wanted to. Yet when-
ever they were alone for more than a few minutes
and the opportunity existed for more than hand-
holding or light kissing, his palms started to sweat
and his mouth went dry. He always felt a weakening

rush of relief when a third party entered the room, and he always did his damnedest to hide it.

At first he'd been confused by his own anxiety, and then angered by it, but by now there was no pretending ignorance of the reason for it. The mortifying but unavoidable truth was that the prospect of real physical intimacy with Jan scared the hell out of him.

Looking down at Jan in his arms, he suddenly knew that he wanted her to accept him as the man he had been before that damned ladder fell out from under him, the man she'd known practically all her life and finally fallen in love with, the man who knew her body so well that his lightest touch could make her purr and moan and whimper with need.

He deepened his kiss, the heel of his hand at her nape and his fingers splayed over the base of her skull. His tongue stiffened to plunge past her teeth, and her breath caught in surprise. She would have pulled away if not for that hard, determined hand at the back of her head. Nick picked up the uncertainty that flickered through her, but he also felt her reluctant response and took heart from it. His right hand began to caress her with a slow, assured touch while the deliberate seduction of his kiss continued until she moaned softly into his mouth. A second later both her hands were clasping his head and her tongue moved against his, stroking and then nudging it back past his lips so that she could take the lead for a while.

The next moan came from Nick's throat, and Jan exulted as she heard it. There had been times during the past six weeks when she'd been afraid she would never hear that low, restless sound again. Ever since she signed the permission forms for Nick's surgery, she'd lived with the dread that no matter what the outcome, he would never completely forgive her for disregarding his wishes. Except for that first morning he hadn't uttered a single accusing word, but that didn't necessarily mean he wasn't still denouncing her as a traitor in his own mind.

She told herself as she responded to the erotic promise of his lips and tongue that he wouldn't be kissing her like this, holding and caressing her like this, if he still felt she'd betrayed him. His fingers brushed the outer curve of her breast, and she shifted slightly to fill his hand with it, reacquaint himself with its shape and size. And then, so swiftly that the breath became trapped in her lungs, he abandoned her breast to seek another, even more sensitive target. His hand adroitly dived under the elasticized waist of her cotton slacks, gliding over her soft lower abdomen and the silky scrap of fabric beyond, coming to rest when it found the damp heat between her legs. His fingers curled to fit his palm to her, and then he pressed upward with such strength and power that Jan felt her torso slide a good inch up his. Her breath finally escaped on a tiny whimpering sound, her lips going slack.

"Nick!" she gasped weakly.

A soft *ping, ping* sounded from the hall, the signal that visiting hours were over for the day. Nick swore softly, and before he could remove his hand Jan arched against it to let him know he wasn't the only one who was disappointed. His fingers squeezed in response, making her shudder and moan helplessly, and then the hand was reluctantly withdrawn.

"We shouldn't have stayed in the lounge for that last hand of poker," he muttered as Jan edged down to lie beside him and tucked her head under his jaw. His heart was racing as fast as hers, and his breathing was just as ragged. She smiled and linked her fingers at the back of his neck.

"Well, how was I to know you were feeling so, um, romantic?"

Nick tilted her head back to lay a soft kiss on her lips, and then another. "Now, if medical science could just come up with a cure for sexual frustration...."

"One already exists," Jan told him, her eyes gleaming with mischief. "It's called a lobotomy. Shall I suggest it to Mac?"

"Bite your tongue! As if I don't have enough problems already!"

Jan laughed and gave him a hard, exuberant kiss, which pushed his head back into the pillow. Her enthusiastic lack of restraint thrilled him, and he looped an arm around her neck to bring her even closer.

"You think you've got problems now?" Jan asked huskily against his mouth. "Sugar, they haven't even started yet. By this time next week you'll be the captive of a love-starved hussy who'll probably keep you locked up in a dark, musty bedroom twenty-four hours a day to satisfy her lascivious cravings, and keep you alive on a diet of peanut butter and whipped cream."

Nick's lips twitched as he stroked an idle finger along the underside of her jaw. "Well," he said quietly, "if this depraved hussy has it in mind to keep me confined to bed, she won't have to bother with chains." His eyes flicked to the wheelchair, and his mouth twisted slightly. "She can just park my wheels on the other side of the room and eliminate any chance of escape."

The sudden bitterness in his voice dismayed Jan. She watched his Adam's apple bob as he swallowed hard, and was devoutly grateful to dear Mac for the advice he'd given her during the past two days. She gently raked her fingers through the hair above Nick's ear and smiled down at him lovingly.

"Hey, the hussy may be a bit depraved, but she's not a monster," she said softly. "Give her a chance. Who knows, you might end up making her *your* prisoner."

Nick's eyes met hers solemnly, his expression betraying nothing. Her fingers stayed buried in his hair, soothing, reassuring while she gazed down at him with a soft smile. A third *ping* was added to the first two, warning all visitors that the nurses had started making the rounds to rout any dawdlers.

"Guess I'd better go," Jan said reluctantly.

"Yeah." Nick's arm was removed from her neck, his hand trailing across her shoulders before it fell to the mattress. Jan pressed another kiss on his lips, then slid off the bed and bent to retrieve her shoes. "Drive carefully," he murmured when she had them on.

"Cross my heart. I should be back by noon tomorrow with your Big Mac." She walked to the door, then turned back to look at him. "I love you," she told him softly.

"Love you, too. Don't forget the extra ketchup."

Jan's smile flashed across the room as she nodded, and then she was gone.

NICK FOLDED HIS HANDS BEHIND HIS HEAD and lay staring up at the ceiling, trying to sort out the different emotions wrangling for supremacy inside him. He felt relief and hope and the lingering vestiges of a passion that had taken him totally by surprise. Why was that? Why had he assumed he wouldn't be capable of feeling desire or passion when he held his wife in his arms; or that if he did, it would be a pale ghost of the real thing? Well, he certainly knew better now. God, he had wanted her! When she started kissing him back and he felt her tongue in his mouth, a bonfire had ignited inside him. He had responded exactly as he always had, except for one thing.

Though he didn't need to look, his gaze lowered, then swept down the front of the silk pajamas Jan had gone out and bought him so he wouldn't have to wear those institutional horrors the hospital provided. The waist of the trousers circled the phantom zone, that area where the feeling faded before vanishing altogether. Above it everything was as it should be: his skin temperature normal, the receptors of his nervous system registering every sensation, even the movement of air when someone passed close by. But below the dividing line, there was nothing. Zilch. The muscles had to be exercised and massaged, the joints flexed, by other people whose hands he couldn't even feel as they manipulated his body to keep it from deteriorating, wasting away.

Therapy was a demoralizing experience for him, but not half as demoralizing as the discovery that Mac's predictions had been right on target. He'd had Jan in his arms, lying almost fully on top of him, and there had been absolutely no physical response where it mattered most, not even a twinge.

Had she known? If she had, how much did it matter to *her*? She'd responded to him, there was no denying that, but it had been a response he'd initially had to wring from her against her better judgment. Yet once she was assured she wasn't going to hurt him, the barriers had come down, finally. He smiled as he remembered the way she'd kissed him back into the pillow, not in the least concerned about the strain she was putting on his neck, and joy was revived by the memory. His eyes drifted closed, and he relived every touch, every taste and scent and labored breath of those precious moments.

BEFORE JAN LEFT THE HOSPITAL she stopped off in the lobby to make a phone call. She spoke briskly to the person at the other end of the line, making her request without offering any explanation for it, then hung up and dug the keys to the Mustang out of her purse on the way to the door. She was troubled about Nick's sensitivity earlier that evening, but she refused to dwell on it. There was a lot to be accomplished in the next few days, and she wasn't even sure how to go about doing half of it.

She unlocked the car and tossed her purse on top of the shopping bag that filled the passenger seat, then ducked to slide behind the wheel. Somehow it would all get done, though, and before Nick was discharged. Her shoulders squared with purpose as she guided the powerful car out of the parking lot and headed for home.

8

ALLEN WAS WAITING AS REQUESTED when she entered the house, comfortably sprawled on the living-room floor in front of her television, a beer in his hand. He deposited it on a table and got up to take the bulky shopping bag she was carrying.

"What's up? Nick hasn't had some kind of setback, has he?"

"Just the opposite," Jan answered with a grin. "He'll be coming home in about another week."

"Hey, terrific! But couldn't you have told me that over the phone? I've been imagining the worst for the past hour and a half."

"Worried sick, were you?" Jan said dryly as she turned off the ball game he'd been watching.

"Well, I had to do something to keep my mind occupied, didn't I? What have you got in this thing, anyway—bricks?"

"No, books." Jan took the bag and dumped its contents onto the cocktail table. "You can start looking through them while I grab a quick shower and change. There's also a list of suggestions from Nick's therapist in there somewhere."

She started for the hall, but Allen stopped her. "Wait a second. What's this all about? Why the portable library?"

"Just start reading," Jan advised. "I'll explain everything after I've had my shower."

While she was wriggling into a kelly-green nightshirt that proclaimed, Adam Was a Rough Draft across the chest, the phone rang.

"Got it!" Allen called, and a minute later he tapped on the bedroom door and announced, "It's Nick."

Jan jerked the door open, her guilty expression making him frown. "Nick!" she repeated in dismay. "What did he say when you answered the phone?"

"'Hello, Allen,'" Allen recited, then added dryly, "He sounded surprised."

Jan didn't doubt it for a minute. She took a deep breath, then picked up the receiver of the extension next to the bed. She'd barely said hello before Nick was demanding, "What's Allen doing there?"

Mentally crossing her fingers, she said the first thing that came to mind. "He saw the lights from his place and thought we might have burglars—can you beat that? Way out here in the boonies? Still, it was sweet of him to check."

"Yeah," Nick said tightly. "Sweet. Thank him nicely and then send him home."

Jan bit her lip. "He's on his way," she said, looking directly into Allen's eyes as he lounged in the doorway. He frowned again, shook his head and then turned around and headed back to the living room.

"Good," Nick's voice said in her ear. It had smoothed out noticeably.

Jan sighed, regretting her deception but regretting even more the necessity for it. "You are an idiot, Nicholas Alexander," she said very softly into the mouthpiece. "But I love you, anyway. And now that you know I got home all right, I want you to tell me good-night, hang up and go to sleep."

There was a brief pause before he responded. "I'll believe you love me when I sink my teeth into that Big Mac you promised. And don't forget—"

"The extra ketchup," Jan finished, a smile in her voice. "Say good-night, Nick."

"Good night, Nick. Oh, and by the way...."

"Yes?" Jan's voice was like liquid silk. She knew what was coming, knew he wouldn't hang up without saying it.

"The idiot loves you, too," he murmured huskily.

When she went back to the living room, modestly wrapped in Nick's short terry robe, Allen handed her a cup of instant coffee. He settled his long frame onto the sofa, then asked quietly, "Want to tell me what that was all about?"

Jan sank down on the carpet. She only hesitated a moment before making up her mind. "He's a little jealous of you."

Allen nearly choked on his beer. "What? You're not serious?"

"Well, maybe jealous is too strong a word," she allowed. "But he does feel threatened by our closeness, and right now he's vulnerable. I just didn't want him lying there tormenting himself with doubts and questions, worrying needlessly. So I told him a couple of white lies," she admitted with an uncomfortable shrug.

Allen stared at her silently for a while. "You know," he said eventually, "this makes me feel just a little uneasy. I mean—" he shifted, gesturing restlessly with one hand "—you knew how he felt when you asked me to meet you here. And now here we sit in his house—"

"It's my house, too," Jan put in quietly.

Allen ignored her. He sat forward, frowning, to trade the almost-empty bottle for one of the books on the table in front of him. "I can't help feeling a little funny about it, that's all. And I know how tough it must be for him now, how frustrated he must get—seeing you walk away when visiting hours are over."

"Yes," Jan agreed somberly. "He does get frustrated—bitterly so, at times." With her index finger she tapped the thick paperback Allen held. "But there are things we can do to help him feel more independent. Did you look through this one?"

Allen turned the book in his hands, nodding. The title, *The Source Book for the Disabled,* seemed to leap off the cover at him in giant blue letters, all capitals.

"It seems very comprehensive. But—" Jan sensed his hesitancy before he lifted troubled eyes to her "—this book, and all the others, well, they're for handicapped people. Nick isn't—"

Her eyes widened in surprise. "No, of course not! Mac still says he'll only need the chair for a couple of months tops, and maybe a cane or walker for a little while after that."

Allen slumped in relief. "Thank God. When I saw all this, I was afraid—" He released a gusty sigh, then picked up his beer again and drained the bottle in one long chug. "So I guess you want me to help get the house ready for his homecoming, huh?"

"That's right. I can make a lot of the arrangements by phone, but I can't be both here and with Nick at the same time—"

"Say no more," Allen interrupted. "I'll do whatever I can."

THE FOLLOWING MORNING Jan stopped by the post office to collect the mail. Sorting through it on the way to the car, she stopped dead in her tracks. She stared down at the heavy cream vellum envelope in her hand with a mixture of fascination and dread. It was one of several letters to Nick, except the return address on this one immediately caught her attention and held her stunned gaze. The letter was from Marina.

She was astonished to realize that she hadn't even spared a thought for the other woman in months—two months, to be precise. Marina Calhoun had barely entered her mind since her wedding night. For a moment Jan wondered what the woman would be writing Nick about, and then she stiffened as she remembered that Marina had been the reason he'd asked her to marry him in the first place. She'd wanted to bring Leslie out for a visit, during which she intended to convince Nick to give marriage to her another try.

Was that what she was writing about—to tell him they were coming and when? Jan felt a surge of bitter anger toward the woman she'd never even met but had both envied and resented for more than ten years. She couldn't come now; not *now*, while Nick was so vulnerable. Dammit, she couldn't!

She fumed all the way back to the hospital, and had actually parked the Mustang and was on her way across the lot before she realized she'd forgotten to get his Big Mac. Cursing under her breath, she returned to the car to go in search of a McDonald's. Half an hour later she carried the mail in one hand and a white sack in the other as she hurried through the main entrance of the hospital.

Nick was just coming down the hall from the lounge when she stepped off the elevator. He smiled as he caught sight of the sack, and Jan's throat unexpectedly went tight. She'd become accustomed to seeing him in pajamas and robe, and by now he controlled the wheelchair so skillfully that she was seldom consciously aware of it. But suddenly she saw him as if for the first time, as if she was Marina, and pity rose inside her. She smothered it at once, afraid he might somehow sense it. Waggling the sack at him with a forced smile, she strode into his room and closed the door behind them.

"I hope you're hungry," she said, as she deposited the stack of mail on the cantilevered table beside the bed and sank down into an armchair. There was another table beside it, and she began removing food from the sack to give herself an extra few moments for composure. "I got you a large order of fries, too."

Nick suddenly appeared in front of her. He set the brake on his chair, then reached out to grasp both her hands, stilling their nervous movements. "I'm hungry, all right," he said in a throaty growl. "But not necessarily for French fries."

The exaggerated lechery in his voice made Jan's head snap up in surprise. Before she could do more than take in the laughter glinting in his eyes he leaned forward, shifting his grip from her hands to her upper arms, and the next thing she knew he was half dragging, half lifting her out of her chair and onto his lap.

"Nick!" she gasped in alarm. "Are you crazy! Your back—"

"Oh, shut up," he murmured. "My back's fine." His arms encircled her to tug her against his chest, and he flashed a wicked grin. "Aren't you going to ask what I *am* hungry for?"

Jan's skirt had ridden up past her knees when he pulled her onto his lap, and she was acutely aware of the smooth texture of his robe under her bare thighs and, beneath it, the solid contours of his legs. He didn't seem to be in any pain, and she *had* longed to be in exactly this position for weeks. She pursed her lips thoughtfully as her arms slid around his neck and she leaned into him.

"Whipped cream?" she guessed with a straight face.

Nick's appreciative chuckle vibrated inside her mouth as his lips came down on hers. For the first few seconds the kiss was soft, tender and sweet. And then Jan's fingers slipped into his hair and she twisted carefully at the waist to press her breasts against him, and any lingering uncertainty Nick felt flew right out the window. He made little growling sounds into her mouth as he sipped at it thirstily, tilting his head first to the left, then the right, his tongue darting out to tease hers with light, fleeting strokes and gentle nudges.

"Mmm, you're delicious," he muttered between nibbling kisses. "I could gobble you up here and now."

One of his hands retreated under her arm, squeezing her ribs before it settled warmly on her breast. A sighing moan whispered past Jan's lips as his lean fingers toyed with her nipple through the thin knit polo shirt she was wearing. She broke out in goose bumps and had to wrench her mouth away from his for a deep, painful breath. Her head fell onto Nick's shoulder, and her breast heaved under his hand.

"Gosh," she panted against his neck, "it's really nice to know I've been missed, but I don't think I can take much more of this on an empty stomach. The room's already spinning."

Nick continued caressing her breast while he gave her a one-armed hug. "Don't tell me—you were so eager to rush back to your loving hubby's waiting arms that you didn't eat breakfast," he murmured, his mouth at her temple.

Jan's lips curved against the warm skin of his throat. "To tell the truth, there wasn't much in the house except beer and peanut butter."

She lifted her head, and her grinning mouth was immediately captured for a hard, determined kiss. "Well, darlin'," Nick drawled as his lips touched her face in half a dozen places, "I'm afraid you'll just have to bear up for a few more minutes. Right now I need this more than either of us needs food."

"Me too," Jan admitted breathlessly as his lips grazed her jaw on the way to her throat. Her head fell back, and she rested against the hard, strong arm waiting to support her.

"Do you mean that?" Though Nick's voice was muffled by her skin, it still came out sounding a little strained.

She shivered deliciously, her fingers clenching in his hair when he nipped gently at her collarbone. "Oh, Nick. You can't possibly know."

"Show me," he urged huskily.

Jan pulled herself upright on his lap, her eyes darkening with concern. "I...." She hesitated, and he held his breath, dread settling in his stomach like a rock. He saw her mouth quiver in a frail, apologetic smile as she confessed, "I'm afraid if I let go, I'll hurt you." And then without warning her arms tightened, and she pressed her cheek to his, hugging his head fiercely. "Oh, darling, I'd rather die than hurt you," she whispered tremulously into his ear.

Relief swept through him, clearing the way for a joy so profound it made him want to laugh and cry at the same time. He released her breast to tenderly clasp the back of her head, swallowing hard.

"You beautiful dunce," he said, and didn't even care that she must hear the emotion in his voice. He rubbed his cheek against hers. "You won't hurt me, promise," he assured her gently. "And I want you to touch me...I need to know that you're not turned off by this damn chair or—"

Jan pressed her fingers against his lips, stopping him. "And you dare to call *me* a dunce!" She clucked her tongue at him in loving rebuke, then removed her fingers to pass it slowly along his lower lip. "Are you sure this doesn't hurt?" she breathed into his mouth as it opened in invitation.

Nick's hands settled at the sides of her waist and his eyes gleamed at her through long, thick lashes. "Positive." His tongue came out to return the sensuous caress. "Does that hurt?"

Jan's laugh was low and rich. "Not a bit. Let's see about this." She ducked her head, and while her teeth administered tiny love bites to his neck and shoulders he felt her hand slide down to the V formed by his robe and pajamas. Tugging impatiently at the top button of the pajamas, she whispered, "Where can I touch you?" She didn't sound the least bit hesitant; in fact, her fingers were already moving through the hair on his chest, her touch light but assertive.

Nick worked the tail of her shirt free, then ran his hands up her ribs until his thumbs brushed the undersides of her breasts. He'd already discovered that she wasn't wearing a bra, and he couldn't help smiling in satisfaction when his touch made her gasp softly.

"Wherever you want," he murmured in answer to her question. His hands each rose another centimeter, then halted. "Where can I touch you?"

Now Jan was using both hands to eliminate the layers of fabric covering his chest, though she hadn't abandoned his neck. He smiled again when a button from his pajamas landed on the floor and bounced twice before rolling under the bed.

"You never felt the need to ask me that before," she mumbled absently. Having managed to separate both pajamas and robe to his waist, her hands wasted no time diving inside. Palms flattened against his smooth, warm skin, fingers spread, they glided around to his back as she released a contented sigh.

"I could say the same about you," Nick admonished gently. "Since when have you asked where I want to be touched? You know what I like, what gives me pleasure. I'm the same man, Janet Faye. I haven't turned into a whole new person, somebody you have to get to know all over again."

She sat back to look at him, wondering if she'd offended his pride by asking. "I just didn't want to do anything you might not be comfortable with," she said gently, then kissed him in apology.

Surprisingly, Nick grinned. "Funny, I don't remember you having any such reservations when you were smearing chunky peanut butter on my—"

"Nick!" Jan's squawk drowned out the last word as she cast a frantic glance toward the hall. "For heaven's sake!"

"Or when you were licking it off, either, for that matter," he went on unabashedly. "I thought you'd never get it all, and by the time you did I was practically a basket case. Lord, woman, you must have the slowest tongue in the West."

His eyes danced with devilish laughter as Jan tried to shush him, until she finally realized how much he was enjoying himself and plastered her mouth on his. Nick's hands closed over her breasts at exactly the same instant. She made a muffled sound that might have been a laugh, and then she was arching into his hands.

"You idiot. What if Mac or one of the nurses had come in while you were taking that little stroll down memory lane?"

"What if Mac or one of the nurses came in *now*?"

he countered. "Think we could pass this off as some kind of therapy?"

Jan chuckled and kissed him hard, then pulled back to look at him adoringly. Her hands were still flattened on his back; his still covered her breasts. They smiled into each other's eyes.

"I can't remember the last time I heard you laugh like that," he said softly.

Jan sighed. Her hands caressed his back in slow, loving circles. "Neither can I. There hasn't been a lot to laugh about in the past six weeks. I guess I haven't been much fun to be around, huh?"

Nick shook his head, suddenly solemn. "You've been wonderful. I'd never have made it without you to lean on, especially in the beginning. You were always there for me, always giving whatever I needed." His mouth tilted wryly. "Sometimes before I even knew I needed it. No matter how worried you were, or how tired, you were always there, and I'll love you forever for that."

Jan drew a shaky breath and blinked a couple of times to disperse the tears that suddenly filled her eyes. "Hey, I was just doing my job," she murmured huskily. "The verbal contract was very specific. I agreed to stick by you through sickness and health, remember?"

"I remember," he said softly. "I know it hasn't been easy for you—*I* haven't been easy. I've been moody and short-tempered, a real pain in the butt at times. Lord knows how you've managed to put up with me, but I promise to do better from now on."

Jan tilted her head to one side as she studied him. She saw a man whose life had been abruptly turned upside down just six short weeks ago; a man whose physical and mental anguish during those weeks she had glimpsed only rarely, when exhaustion created

chinks in the armor of his pride. Yet he had refused
to surrender to the despair that must have been
his constant companion. At that moment her love
swelled to such proportions that she felt almost
weightless, as if she might float right up to the ceiling.

"What are you thinking?" Nick asked quietly.

She closed the distance between them to brush her
lips across his. "Just that I exhibited remarkably good
judgment for a ten-year-old." When he frowned in
confusion, she clarified the statement. "In deciding
that you were the man I was going to marry."

"The hell you say!" he declared with a surprised
laugh. "You mean my fate was sealed all along?"

"From day one," Jan confirmed smugly. "You
never stood a chance. It took fifteen years, but you're
finally mine, and I intend to see that you never forget it. Well?" she challenged when he just sat there
grinning at her. "Don't you have anything to say?
No rebuttal, no snappy comeback?"

Nick's hands suddenly left her breasts to slide
around to her back. He hauled her against his chest,
his grin transforming to a tender smile as he bent to
her mouth. "I'll keep my remarks brief and to the
point," he whispered against it. "Amen and hallelu-
jah!"

His kiss was warm and ardent, but more affectionate than impassioned, more playful than seductive.
He kissed her as if she was his best friend as well as
his lover. It was wonderful. And then a loud rum-
bling from Jan's stomach caused him to break away
with a throaty chuckle.

She grinned sheepishly. "Well, I told you I didn't
have any breakfast."

She stayed on his lap while they demolished the
cold food, feeding one another soggy French fries

dripping with ketchup so that they could take turns licking the excess off each other's mouths. Because they stopped so often to laugh or nuzzle or just exchange silly adolescent smiles, it took twice as long as it normally would have to finish eating. But eventually all that remained of the meal were a couple of Big Mac boxes, two French-fry containers and a pile of flattened ketchup packets.

"I must say," Jan remarked as she stuffed the litter back into the sack, "you're in an exceptionally fine mood today. I can't remember when I heard *you* laugh this much, either. Is there any special reason, other than my scintillating company, that is?"

"Well...." Nick's expression became suspiciously bland as he ran a lazy finger down her nose. "I did have a rather pleasant surprise this morning, while I was down in therapy."

Jan shoved the sack in the direction of the table, no longer teasing as she gazed into his eyes with barely suppressed excitement.

"What? Tell me."

His shrug was negligent. "It's nothing much, really. I've got another four centimeters of feeling back, that's all."

"*Nick!*" Her arms flew around his neck and she rained joyous kisses all over his face. "You rotten louse, why didn't you tell me right away?"

An exuberant laugh rumbled up from his chest as he captured her head to hold her still for an extended, breath-stealing fusion of lips and tongues.

"I was waiting for just the right time, and then we started necking and I sort of got sidetracked."

Jan pulled back a little to demand, "Show me."

He took her hand and began moving it slowly down his chest. "Right about—" her fingers passed his lower abdomen, and then the waist of his pajamas, and Jan realized she was holding her breath ''—there,'' he murmured as he pressed her palm to the hard ridge of his pelvis.

She was instantly ashamed of the brief stab of disappointment she felt. To atone for the selfish reaction she curled her fingers to firmly grasp his hip.

"You can really feel that?" she asked, squeezing lightly.

Nick's eyelids flickered, then steadied. "Oh, yeah," he said in a husky voice. "In fact, it doesn't entirely stop there. Below my hips it's more a sensation of pressure than actual touch, but the feeling's definitely coming back. Of course I still can't move anything, but Mac says it's just a matter of time."

There was a note of relief in his voice that surprised Jan. She sat very still as she gazed deep into his eyes, trying to see beyond them and into his mind.

"You've never really believed that until now, though, have you?" she asked softly. "You've never completely accepted that this is only a temporary condition, that eventually you'll be able to get out of this chair and walk again."

For an instant pain appeared in Nick's eyes before he lowered his lashes to screen them from her. His mouth quirked cynically. "You know me, the eternal skeptic."

"Oh, Nick!" Her heart ached for him, for the agony he must have suffered silently in the past six weeks. "You mean that all this time— It must have been terrible for you."

Then, in an emotional about-face, she settled her head into the curve of his shoulder with a contented little smile. "But thank goodness that's all behind us now. By this time next week we'll be home again. I can hardly wait."

"Neither can I," Nick murmured in tender amusement. "Home sweet home. Just you and me and the depraved hussy." Jan pulled her hand away from his hip and punched his chest. He grinned. "I've always wondered what it would be like to have two gorgeous woman vying for my favors."

"Who said the hussy was gorgeous?"

"Okay. I'll settle for one gorgeous and one depraved." Ignoring her indignant snort, he hugged her tight. "Or one who's both, and has the added attraction of being my gutsy, loving wife. Just think, hours and days and weeks of peace and solitude, with no breakfast trays being shoved at me at 6:00 A.M., and no infernal bell driving you out at night, and best of all, no other people! After the past six weeks, I'm *really* ready to turn into a recluse."

Jan chuckled. "You're forgetting the therapist Mac's lined up. She'll be out every day. And I'd bet my last dollar that my mother will hightail it out here to 'lend a hand' just as soon as she knows when you're being released."

Her amusement suddenly vanished, her eyes clouding with anxiety. Nick asked what was wrong, but instead of answering she eased off his lap and went to fetch Marina's letter from the stack of mail she'd brought. She handed it to him with a grim frown.

"And maybe two uninvited houseguests."

Nick glanced down at the envelope, and his lips compressed in anger. "Hell," he muttered. He read the letter without commenting, and by the time he finished his face was creased in sardonic amusement. "Well, I'll be damned. Leave it to Marina."

"What does she say?" Jan wanted to know. "Are they coming or not?"

"Here, read it for yourself." He handed her the

letter, and as her eyes raced down the single sheet of paper, her mouth fell open.

"She's married!"

"Apparently she found herself a bigger fish," Nick said dryly. "The name might not mean anything to you, but he's Hollywood's latest wunderkind, the 'new Spielberg.' She's probably counting on him to make her a star. He's about a dozen years younger than Marina and reported to be quite a ladies' man. She'd better watch him around Leslie, or she's liable to find herself in a real bind."

Jan sank down on the armchair beside him as relief washed through her. "Well," she remarked casually as she refolded the letter and put it back in the envelope, "this would seem to eliminate your need for a wife to protect you from darling Marina. Since my services will no longer be required, I guess I'll just drop you off at the house, collect my things and start looking for another job."

"Like hell," Nick growled. He seized her wrist to yank her toward him, at the same time leaning forward. "Make no mistake, Pocahontas," he murmured when their faces were less than an inch apart, "both you *and* your services are most definitely needed, and will be for a long, *long* time."

"Oh." Jan gave in to an impish grin. "Well, I suppose that's just as well. There *is* the matter of an interrupted honeymoon. Of course I guess you could give me a couple of weeks' severance pay instead."

Nick muttered something unintelligible as he closed the distance between them. He kissed her sensuously, deeply, and ignored the small voice that insisted this was the time to tell her—to prepare her, give her fair warning that the "honeymoon" might not be resumed quite as soon as she anticipated. He wouldn't be released for another week, and who could say what might happen before then?

As JAN HAD PREDICTED, her mother announced that she would fly out to stay with them for at least the first few days Nick was home. Jan tried to tactfully suggest that they would welcome some time alone, but her subtlety was completely wasted. Dolores was convinced that "the children" would need her, and no amount of diplomatic discouragement would convince her otherwise. She was coming, and that was that.

For the past six weeks time had dragged, sometimes seeming to hang suspended for hours, even days. Now, for both Nick and Jan, it seemed to have accelerated drastically. Almost before they could take it in, Mac had signed the official release and Nick was free to leave the hospital. Jan went down to take care of the bill while a nurse helped him dress in clothes Jan had collected on her last trip home.

She felt nervous, jittery, on edge. One moment she told herself it was perfectly natural, an inevitable effect of the tension she'd been under for so long. The next moment she knew better, and the knowledge agitated her even more. Nick was finally coming home! She'd expected to feel elated, relieved, even impatient — but certainly not anxious. The main reason for the anxiety was the long talk she and Mac had had the day before. So much of Nick's recovery seemed to hinge on his attitude, his emotional orientation. And *her* attitude and behavior, especially during the first day or two, could have a radical effect on his, on how well he adjusted to the move from hospital to home. In a way she wished Mac had left well enough alone and not tried to counsel her at all. She sighed heavily as she waited for the elevator, which would take her back up to Nick's floor. All she could do was take things as they came and hope for the best.

FOR THE PAST TWENTY-FIVE MILES or so Nick had been lying back with the bucket seat in a half-reclining position, eyes closed. He wasn't asleep, nor was he particularly tired, despite Jan's concern about his making the trip by car.

The fuss she'd made over their travel arrangements had caused an uneasy anger in Nick. He didn't want her treating him like some frail, helpless invalid who needed caring for, looking after. Yet he was aware that his reaction had probably been exaggerated, and he was also aware of the reason. He'd grown increasingly tense during the past few days, so that the least little thing seemed to get under his skin. So many questions plagued him: would he cope all right, once he was home? Not just with the day-to-day problems of mobility, but emotionally? He was determined to be as independent as possible, yet he had to be realistic. There were going to be times when he'd need help with some simple task he'd always been able to accomplish without any trouble at all. Would he be able to let Jan give him that help without feeling humiliated or resentfully angry? And what about her—how were the next few weeks going to affect her feelings for him, if at all?

"Are you asleep?" she asked softly, ending his self-absorption and making him feel guilty for ignoring her.

He put his hands on the smooth vinyl seat and stretched the slight stiffness out of his back, arching his neck with a lethargic grunt. "No, just resting."

Then, because he didn't want her to think he'd been in need of a rest already, he added, "I'd forgotten how boring it can get when you're not the one doing the driving."

Jan smiled and reached over to take his hand. "Good news—the boring part's over." She turned the wheel easily with one hand and the Mustang drifted into the driveway and glided to a smooth stop in front of the garage door. "We're home," she announced unnecessarily.

He barely had time for the fact to register before the front door opened and both Dolores and Allen were hurrying toward the car. Jan slipped out her side without his even noticing, and as Allen opened his door she appeared beside him, pushing the wheelchair she'd somehow already unloaded from the back seat and brought around.

"Hey, welcome home, hotshot," Allen said with a grin.

"Yes, welcome home!" Dolores echoed from behind him. She was smiling from ear to ear.

Jan laughed. "If you two don't mind, could we have the reunion inside?" she suggested. "If Nick's as hot and tired as I am, he could probably be persuaded to celebrate his homecoming with a cold beer."

Nick glanced up at her, and the warmth of her smile rivaled that of the sun beating down on the car roof. He smiled back and impulsively drawled, "I knew there was a reason I keep you around." The instantaneous flare in her eyes told him she remembered: it was the same thing he'd said the day he returned from New York, the day he'd asked her to marry him.

Jan's smile became soft and intimate for a moment before she forced herself to tear her gaze from his and turned to Dolores. "Mother, would you mind taking my suitcase inside while I put the car in the garage?"

It didn't occur to her until she closed the trunk lid and saw Allen settling Nick in the chair that he might need any assistance in getting out of the car. At the hospital the orderly had stood back and offered a few helpful suggestions, but let Nick make the transfer himself. Of course the bucket seat was quite a bit lower than the seat of the chair.... She bit her lip in distress. If he had needed help, it should have come from her, not Allen.

Dolores gave her a gentle prod from behind. "Get with it, Janet. Go ahead and put the car away. We'll take Nick inside. Oh, I can't wait to see his face when he finds out what all you two have done!"

A sudden chill enveloped Jan, lifting the hair at her nape and raising goose bumps on her arms. At the same time she experienced an alarming feeling of dread, almost a premonition of impending disaster. Telling herself she was being ridiculous, that the disaster had been averted seven weeks ago, she gave herself a mental shake and went to open the garage door.

For the next several minutes Nick was bombarded by Dolores's excited chatter and Allen's enthusiastic commentary as they took him inside to show off all the changes that had been made in preparation for his arrival. The first of them, the ramp at the front door, made him smile with gratitude at someone's—probably Jan's—thoughtfulness. Once inside, however, Allen kept control of the chair as he hustled Nick past the living room and down the hall, and the gratitude gave way to an inexplicable sense of foreboding. And then they reached the bedroom door, and the foreboding was replaced by a sick, sinking feeling in the pit of his stomach.

By the time Jan joined the two of them in the bedroom, he was struggling to subdue his rising panic. It was all he could do not to recoil when she came to him, smiling as she held out a frosty bottle of beer.

"Well, are you surprised?" she asked, still smiling.

Nick lifted the bottle to his mouth to conceal the way it contorted. "Oh, yeah," he murmured, somehow managing to keep the bitterness out of his voice. "I'm surprised, all right."

You lied to me! You, Mac, all of you, all along. Damn you, you lied!

They must have. Otherwise, why had she had all this *hardware* installed? The ramps, the grab bars, the trapeze at the head of the bed—all of it! You didn't go to all this trouble, make such extensive modifications to a house for somebody who was only going to need them for three or four weeks. Which meant they'd been lying all along, feeding him hope, when they knew there was none.

He wasn't ever going to walk again. He was going to spend the rest of his life in this damned chair—and Jan had known it from the beginning.

9

THERE WAS NO NEED to torture himself wondering why. He knew why.

He had provided the motivation for Jan's deceit when he told her he'd rather be dead than crippled for life. What else could she have done but lie? He'd put her in an impossible position, he understood that; but understanding didn't mean he could forgive her. Unfair and irrational that might be, but it was how he felt. The sense of betrayal went too deep to allow forgiveness. He wheeled himself into the bathroom, unable to keep his emotions in check.

He remembered how warm, how lovingly demonstrative she'd been while he was in the hospital, and felt sick at the thought that that, too, had been part of the deception. Had she forced herself to let him hold her, kiss and caress her, even going so far as to fake a response to keep him from guessing the truth? Dear God, how could he believe in anything, if he couldn't believe in Jan?

He took a few minutes to regain control over his facial expression before rejoining the others. When he did, another surprise awaited him. Once again Allen took control of his chair, pushing it down the ramp at the rear door and across the patio to the bungalow behind the house. All the furniture had been removed from the living room, and a minigymnasium installed. His therapy would take place out here, Jan informed him cheerfully. He bit back the urge to ask why the hell he should bother keeping up with the therapy when they all knew it would be a waste of time. He didn't trust himself to confront her with his accusations just yet.

Jan had been aware of the drastic change in Nick's mood from the instant he took the bottle of beer. He was wound as tight as the mainspring of a five-dollar watch, holding everything together by sheer strength of will. As the afternoon wore on, she wondered, should she do or say something to ease the strain he was under, and if so, what?

Allen stayed for dinner. He used the gas grill on the patio to cook steaks, and Dolores insisted on taking care of everything else. Jan suspected they were giving her and Nick some time to sit back and relax, get used to being in their own home again.

Except it wasn't working. Nick didn't relax; if anything, he became even more hostile and withdrawn when they were alone in the living room. It occurred to Jan that the trip might have taken more out of him than he was willing to admit. She worked up her nerve and hesitantly asked if he was tired. Nick's denial was sharp, his voice filled with resentment that she should even ask. Yet at nine o'clock he brusquely announced that he was going to bed. Jan automatically rose to go with him, but the look he gave her froze her to the spot.

"There's no need for you to come," he told her in a tone as frigid as the expression in his eyes. "Stay and visit with Allen and your mother."

It seemed to Jan that there had been an additional coating of ice on Allen's name, but it wasn't something she could question him about in front of the others.

She sank back into the chair she'd just vacated. "All right, if you're sure. But if you need any help—"

"I won't," Nick interrupted curtly. Without another word to any of them, he turned his chair and headed for the bedroom. There was a barely restrained violence in every thrust his hands gave the wheels.

After he'd gone Jan glanced at her mother, then Allen. Dolores was frowning slightly, her smooth forehead puckered over the bridge of her nose. Allen looked much more upset.

"It's been a long day," Jan said into the awkward silence. "And an exhausting one, both physically and emotionally."

Dolores nodded, her frown vanishing. "And this isn't the way he'd have preferred to come home."

"No. Mac warned me he might have to go through a period of adjustment." It was to Allen that Jan directed an appealing look tinged with apology. "We'll just have to be patient, give him some time."

Allen's eyes were troubled as they met hers. He was thinking of the expression on Nick's face when he saw what they'd done to the bungalow. He'd looked as if he'd like to set a torch to the place or level it to the ground with a bulldozer. He remembered his own spontaneous reaction to the literature Jan had brought home, and a dreadful suspicion began to take shape in his mind. What if Nick had taken one look at all this stuff and jumped to the same conclusion he'd jumped to when he saw those books? He should have said something to Jan at the time, should have voiced his reservations. But he hadn't, and now the damage appeared to have been done. To say anything now would be like closing the barn door after the horse was gone.

"Right," he agreed, infusing an optimism he didn t feel into his voice. "He just needs a little time to adjust. He'll probably snap out of it in a couple of days." He gave Jan an encouraging smile and hoped against hope that it really would work out that way.

Shortly after that, Allen left. By the time Jan and Dolores had finished washing the dishes and tidying the kitchen, it was nearly ten. Still, Jan loitered, cleaning the top of the already-gleaming range, sweeping nonexistent crumbs off the floor, finding any number of ways to put off the inevitable—until Dolores plucked a Brillo pad out of her hand and shoved her toward the door.

"He ought to be in bed by now. Go on, before you rub a hole in that pan."

Jan's mouth tilted ruefully as she leaned over to kiss her mother on the cheek. "Okay, okay, I'm going. If you hear any unusual noises, like blood-curdling screams, or the sounds of furniture splintering—"

"I'll stuff cotton in my ears. Vamoose, Janet Faye. Hasn't it occurred to you that he might be wondering why you're still out here, when he's in there?" she asked gently.

From the startled look in Jan's eyes, it obviously hadn't. "Oh, mother," she murmured fervently, "what would I do without you?"

Dolores's smile was benign. "Don't be melodramatic, Janet. We both know you do just fine without me. Now, scoot! And for pity's sake, don't put on one of those sexless nightshirts you're so fond of," she added as she turned away to rinse the skillet Jan had been scouring.

Jan slipped into the room as quietly as she could, just in case Nick might already be asleep. It was impossible to tell if he was or not; there wasn't a sound or a movement from the humped shape occupying his side of the bed. She eased open the drawer containing her underwear and nightgowns and rummaged among the garments until she found what she was searching for. Then, smiling to herself, she hurried into the bathroom, piling her hair on top of her head before taking a quick shower.

Nick still hadn't stirred or made a sound when she lifted the sheet and slipped into bed. Telling herself that he needed a good night's sleep, she sighed in resignation and turned onto her side, facing him. One hand inched across the mattress until it encountered his warm flesh, and then her fingers climbed his side to settle softly on the flat plateau of his stomach. She smiled as her eyes drifted closed. He hadn't wasted any time getting rid of the silk pajamas.

Suddenly Nick's hand closed on her wrist, and he flung her arm back to her side of the bed with such force that Jan was dumbfounded for several seconds. When she recovered, she raised up on one elbow to stare at him in hurt surprise.

"Nick!" It was half admonition and half injured lament. He just kept staring fixedly at the ceiling, his face in profile harsh and unrelenting. "What on earth...?" Jan began indignantly, then forced herself to calm down and began again. "I thought you were asleep."

"Obviously I wasn't." The sarcasm in his voice could have been cut with a knife.

"Obviously." There was a trace of acerbity in her tone, as well. "But that's hardly any reason—"

"I'd appreciate it if you'd refrain from groping around under the covers when you think I won't be aware of it, or at any other time, for that matter."

Jan was too shocked, and then too incensed by the accusation to take notice of the savage bitterness with which it was voiced.

"Groping!" she repeated on an outraged gasp.

"*Groping!* How dare you use that word! What on earth's wrong with you? I only wanted—"

Nick's head turned on the pillow, and she was instantly silenced by the blazing fury in his eyes.

"I know exactly what you wanted," he said, his voice low and deadly with rage. "But I won't have you 'checking me out,' satisfying your morbid curiosity like I was some kind of freak."

For a moment Jan was too stunned to reply, and then she realized what he'd said, what he thought, and the blood drained from her face.

"Nick!" she whispered wretchedly. "Oh, God... no, darling, *no*! I wasn't—"

But he didn't allow her to finish. "Why don't I spare us both any further embarrassment?" he grated, his voice cold now and very, very quiet, as if he was directing every ounce of self-control toward his vocal cords. "Physically, everything's still intact, and there are no tubes, bags or other 'appliances.' But that's not really what you wanted to know, is it, my love?" The sneering emphasis he gave the last two words made Jan flinch involuntarily, and his mouth twisted when he saw it. "The answer to the question you can't bring yourself to ask outright is no, I can't."

For just an instant his control slipped, and his voice became hoarse. Sympathetic pain lanced through Jan, but when she impulsively reached out to him his rejection was even more violent than the first time.

"Don't!" he said between clenched teeth as he shoved her hand away. "For God's sake, leave me some dignity!" He drew a rasping breath and jerked his hand from hers as if she'd scorched him. "Don't touch me, Jan," he said with cold deliberation. "Just don't touch me."

Jan wallowed in uncertainty as she lay rigidly silent beside him. One part of her told her that he was at the end of his rope and that to push him, put any more strain on his already ragged control, would be unforgivably cruel. But another part was urging her to throw her arms around him whether he wanted that or not and hang on for dear life, until he was forced to accept whatever comfort she could give.

As she hesitated, another emotion joined the pain and regret churning inside her: anger. It sizzled and popped in her brain, fizzed behind her eyes. Damn his thick-headed pride, *and* his utterly selfish attitude! So he was in pain, his ego suffering. Did that give him the right to attack her so viciously? She had feelings, too, and if he thought she'd put up with this kind of treatment for long, he had another think coming.

"All right, Nick," she murmured, her voice ominously soft, her narrowed eyes on his averted face. "I get the message. I won't lay a finger on you. Of course I can't guarantee not to accidentally bump into you in my sleep. I suppose you'd prefer me to sleep on the sofa?" The last dig was loaded with undisguised sarcasm.

A muscle jumped in Nick's cheek, but he didn't meet her eyes. "As a matter of fact, yes, I would," he replied bluntly, and Jan's eyes flew wide in reaction.

"Well, that's just too damned bad! This happens to be my bed, too, and I'm not about to move out of it just to spare your precious male pride. You don't want to share it with me—fine, *you* go sleep on the couch, because I'm not budging!"

And with that, she flounced onto her left side, presenting her back to him as she punched her pillow into shape.

"Good night!" she snapped, and then for good measure added a pithy and patently insincere, "And sweet dreams!"

Even if those parting shots hadn't been calculated to discourage any reply, Nick would have been incapable of making one. She had thrown his mind into total confusion with her display of righteous anger. Where was the guilty remorse he'd expected, the pity he'd dreaded? Good Lord, you'd think *he* was the one in the wrong! The outburst seemed to have drained her, or maybe purged her, because in a very short time her shallow, regular breathing told him she was sound asleep. He felt a surge of irritation. How could she just drop off like that, as if she didn't have a blessed thing on her conscience? That thought alone kept him wide awake for another two hours.

When Jan awoke she was snuggled up at Nick's side, the sheer white gown she'd bought for her wedding night twisted and bunched around her thighs. She spent a lovely few minutes just enjoying the feel of him next to her. Apparently she wasn't the only one whose antagonism had slipped away in sleep; Nick's left arm was under her, his hand resting lightly but possessively on her hip. She smiled and edged closer to place a soft kiss at the corner of his mouth. He stirred, and she kissed him there again. His eyes opened halfway. They were still shadowed with sleep, soft and not quite focused.

"Good morning," Jan whispered just before her mouth settled on his.

"Morning," he responded in a rusty murmur against her lips.

Deciding that was enough conversation for the time being, Jan opened her mouth and lifted her left hand to his chest. Her fingers lingered briefly, then moved on to his neck, eventually burying themselves in the thick hair over his ear.

After a moment or two of soft testing, Nick's lips firmed and both his arms came around her. Murmuring a husky endearment, he slid a hand under her hair at the nape, and the kiss deepened with the beginnings of desire.

And then he was abruptly pushing her away. Jan didn't resist, nor did she protest against his rejection this time. She gazed down at the harsh bitterness etched on his features and rolled away from him with a disgusted sigh.

She climbed off the bed and raked her fingers through her hair before she turned to look at him.

"I'll give you three days," she announced flatly. A frown line appeared between Nick's brows, but he didn't speak. "For that length of time you can sulk, or pout, feel sorry for yourself all you want." His mouth thinned at that, but still he remained silent. Jan narrowed her eyes to level a penetrating stare at him.

"Three days," she repeated, enunciating each word clearly. "After that, you take me on at your own risk."

She saw the astonished resentment that last statement provoked just before she turned away to collect some clothes, and smiled. She was humming as she closed the bathroom door behind her. When she emerged ten minutes later, Nick was sitting up in bed, gripping the trapeze as he prepared to transfer to the chair. His lips twisted in a cynical smile as she approached the foot of the bed. He waited, certain she'd offer to help him and anticipating the pleasure he'd derive from telling her exactly what she could do with her "help." But she didn't offer. His smile vanished.

"Just in time for the first performance of the day,"

he jeered as he placed his other hand on the chair's seat.

Jan tossed her hair back over her shoulder and smiled sweetly. "Gee, too bad I'll miss it. I'll get breakfast started. Hustle your fanny, Alexander, or you'll eat cold eggs."

She was already striding toward the door as she spoke the last words. Nick stared after her with an expression of baffled pique on his face for a full two minutes before he got moving. He'd show her, dammit!

ALLEN CAME OVER at least once a day, ostensibly to bring the mail and take care of any odd jobs that needed doing. Actually, he was constantly monitoring the emotional climate, particularly the tension between Nick and Jan, which seemed to have escalated to the status of an armed truce. Unaware that he held himself at least partially responsible for the situation, Jan confided in him candidly. Though he fretted and stewed, Allen couldn't quite bring himself to do likewise.

On the evening of Nick's second full day home, they were seeing to some routine pool maintenance. Allen replaced a filter cover, wiped his hands on a rag and ambled over to where Jan was vacuuming the sides. Not really sure he wanted to know, he asked casually, "How goes the war?"

She shot him a sardonic look. "We had several minor skirmishes today. Frankly, it's getting harder and harder not to let him get to me. Thank goodness I only have to hang on for one more day...if I last that long. I'm about ready to feed him his word processor, microchip by microchip."

"Do you think he suspects what you're doing?"

Jan snorted as she began to pull in the hose and

coil it around her arm. "Not a chance. It's working even better than I'd hoped. He's so busy trying to get under my skin that he barely has a thought to spare for anything else, including himself. It's turned into a battle of wills, and he's devoting all his time and energy to winning. But he won't," she added with a confident grin. "I positively refuse to be drawn into battle until the three days are up."

"And then?" Allen asked with ill-concealed anxiety. Jan merely smiled, but the quality of the smile caused him to emit a sickly groan. She laughed and impulsively flung her free arm around his neck, pulling him down so she could kiss his cheek.

"Don't worry, I promise not to let you get caught in the cross fire."

"I wonder why I don't feel reassured," Allen muttered. But when she laughed again his lips quirked in a halfhearted smile, and he gave her a brief, affectionate squeeze.

Neither of them was aware that two pairs of eyes were trained on them from the house; nor did they hear the crash when Nick's arm suddenly swept across a table in the living room, sending three magazines, a heavy pewter ashtray and a leaded glass candy dish flying. Dolores was no more than thirty feet away, in the kitchen, and she did hear. Sighing heavily, she turned away from the sink and the window above it and walked with slow reluctance to the door leading into the living room.

Nick had spun his chair away from the patio door just before he cleared the tabletop beside him. Now he sat with his back to the door and the view beyond it, obviously struggling to subdue some powerful emotion. Dolores thought she could guess what that emotion was. She hesitated only a moment before entering the room. Taking a chair almost directly in front of him, she blithely ignored the articles littering the floor. The candy dish, miraculously, hadn't broken.

"There's nothing there," she said quietly, but with unwavering conviction. Nick didn't respond. His gaze seemed riveted to his fists, which lay clenched in his lap.

"Maybe I should say there's nothing there yet." She knew by the tensing of his jaw that he hadn't missed the slight emphasis she put on the last word. "I know my daughter," she went on in a conversational tone. "She'll only take so much of the abuse you've been handing out with such relish. After a while, she'll do one of two things. She'll either murder you, or she'll leave you. Frankly, I don't care to be a witness in either case."

She collected the things he'd knocked off the table and replaced them in an untidy pile, the candy dish nesting precariously in the ashtray, which sat on top of the magazines.

"Looks like you've got some tidying up to do," she commented dryly. "And the biggest mess is inside your own thick skull. I'll leave you to it. I've got a plane reservation to make."

A few minutes later Dolores left the house. Nick watched through the patio door as she approached Jan. Whatever her mother said to her wasn't well received—he could tell that even at this distance. Jan's frown looked ominous as she stared toward the house, but she didn't march across the patio to immediately confront him, as he half expected her to. Instead she waited until they were alone in their room that night. Nick had already bathed and was sitting up in bed, reading, when she came in. A deep-down ache he hadn't even been aware of until then seemed to suddenly ease when he saw the outright animosity in her expression. She closed the door and leaned back against it.

"I hope you're satisfied," she said, wasting no time on preliminaries. "Mother's leaving in the morning."

"I didn't ask her to go," Nick said flatly.

"Of course you didn't," she mocked. "You just made staying in this house intolerable, with your childish sulking and tantrum-throwing."

Nick's eyes narrowed defensively. "Dolores told you that?"

"No," Jan mumbled irritably. She stepped away from the door to collect a nightshirt from the chest of drawers. "What she said was that she was clearing out before the excrement hit the fan."

She shot an accusing look at him and caught him squelching a grin. "Except she didn't use the word 'excrement,'" he ventured with a twinkle in his eyes.

Jan quickly controlled her own lips' tendency to twitch, and frowned at him. "The word she used isn't important. What *is* important is that you've driven her away. I can't say I blame her for leaving, either. The garbage you've been dispensing lately would make any sane person want to avoid you like the plague."

"Including you?" Nick asked smoothly. His eyes were half closed to hide their anticipatory gleam.

"Including me!" Jan shot back instantly.

He lifted one shoulder in a careless shrug. "So don't take it. You can always leave, too."

Jan's eyes widened, then narrowed, until they were little more than slits. Minutes passed in total silence while she stared at him intently, mulling over that last remark.

"Is that the idea?" she asked at length. "First you

get rid of mother and then me; is that how it's supposed to go? Then you could indulge yourself in self-pity and bitterness twenty-four hours a day, and there wouldn't be anybody around to spoil your fun. You think I'm not aware of the resentment you feel toward me, and the reason for it?" She laughed, but there was no humor in the sound. "Oh, I know, all right. But I'll tell you something—if I had it all to do over again, I wouldn't do a single thing any differently. I did what I had to do, what *you* would have done, in my place. If you're honest you'll admit that, if only to yourself."

She paused a moment, her lips pursed as she looked down at the green nightshirt clutched in her hands, then raised her eyes to him again. They were troubled, but filled with a steely determination that warmed Nick's heart.

"So you can go right on sulking and glowering. Snap and snarl at me to your heart's content. It won't change a thing, and it *won't* get rid of me. Heaven knows why, but I still love you, and I'm damned if I'll let you destroy our marriage without putting up one hell of a fight."

She turned abruptly, not giving him a chance to respond to the declaration, and went into the bathroom to get ready for bed. When she came out, the room was in darkness. Nick didn't speak until she'd slipped under the sheet and stopped squirming around to get comfortable. She ended up on her stomach, her face turned away from him. He smiled when he heard her noisy sigh.

"I thought I was supposed to have three days' grace," he drawled.

"Shut up, Nick!"

His smile widened at the curt impatience in her

voice. Oh, yes, her temper was definitely alive and well.

"But that's what you said, that for three days—"

"I'm warning you, Nicholas," Jan growled into her pillow. "It's late and I'm tired. I've also got an upset stomach from excesses of sun and your obnoxious behavior. Don't start on me. I'm not in the mood."

"Just as well," he muttered half under his breath.

Jan bit her lower lip as delight bubbled up inside her. There hadn't been a trace of bitterness in the loaded remark, or sarcasm, either. What there *had* been, thrilling her to her toes, was a hefty dose of the wry humor she'd begun to think he might never display again. She was smiling happily as she burrowed deeper into the pillow and closed her eyes.

ALLEN VOLUNTEERED TO DRIVE DOLORES to the airport the next morning. While Dolores checked the spare room to make sure she hadn't forgotten anything, he and Jan took her luggage out to his Jeep.

"Everything okay?" Allen was frowning slightly as he asked.

"A-okay." Jan smiled fondly, touched by his concern.

"Sure? I thought your mother planned to stay longer than this." Implied in the statement was his fear that without Dolores to run interference, things might quickly go from bad to worse.

Jan linked her arm with his and started leading him toward the front door. "Yes, well, I think she decided we need to be alone to work things out, and she's probably right. Don't look so gloomy, Allen. The war shows definite signs of winding down." She reinforced the claim with an impish grin and a wink, and Allen had to content himself with hoping she was right.

After Allen and Dolores had gone, Nick went out to the bungalow and Jan to the kitchen, to wash the breakfast dishes. When that was done, she dragged out the vacuum cleaner to give the living room a quick once-over. Nick's therapist, a tall, muscular woman named Stella, arrived at nine, just as Jan finished and was rewinding the cord.

"Hi, Stel. He's already out there. He went out about half an hour ago."

"Great!" Stella said with a toothy grin. "I just love to see that kind of enthusiasm. Sometimes I have to all but drag a patient to the exercise table, then stand over him with a whip and a chair to get any work out of the turkey."

Jan laughed, but looking at the woman, she didn't doubt that Stella would be capable of wrestling a fully grown man into line, if she had to.

"Whew, what a workout!" Stella remarked when she stopped by the house at the end of the ninety-minute session. "At the rate he's going, he'll be ready to run the four-forty in another month." She collected her purse from an end table and began fishing for her car keys. "I told him I'd like him to start swimming laps this afternoon, if he's not too tired. But keep an eye on him so he doesn't overdo it, will you, Jan? Otherwise he's liable to be too sore to get out of bed in the morning."

Stella left, and after fifteen minutes had passed and Nick still hadn't come back to the house, Jan went out to the bungalow to see what was keeping him. When he went out, he'd been wearing a gray warm-up suit over blue running shorts. Either he or Stella had removed everything but the shorts for the therapy session. Jan's heart thumped against her

ribs and her stomach did somersaults at the sight of
his sweat-dampened, nearly nude body. How long
had it been since she'd seen that much of him all at
once? Too long, the frustrated wife in her answered
fervently—much, much too long.

She busied herself picking up the warm-up suit
and his slippers to give herself time to get a grip on
her baser urges. When she thought she could look at
him without drooling, she turned and asked with a
casualness she was justifiably proud of, "Are you
about ready for lunch?"

Nick picked up a hand towel from a stack beside
the exercise table and rubbed it over his face. "That
depends," he said as he draped the towel around his
neck. He grasped the ends with both hands and
stared hard into her eyes. "Will Allen be joining
us?"

"Allen?" Jan repeated with a puzzled frown.
"Why would he come back here for lunch?"

Nick's mouth thinned in a satisfied smile that
she'd taken the bait so readily. "Why?" he mocked,
his tone cynical. "Come on, Jan. I've been watching
the two of you. You obviously can't keep your hands
off each other."

"*What?*" At first she was too stunned to do more
than utter the single incredulous squawk. But in a
matter of milliseconds the shock wore off and a
blinding rage took its place.

"Why, you filthy-minded— How *dare* you!"

So angry that she hardly knew what she was doing, she picked up one of his slippers and fired it at
him. Nick hastily ducked to one side, but her aim
had been so accurate that the soft leather shoe
bounced off the side of his head, just above his left
ear.

Jan's hand closed on the other slipper, but before

she could throw it, too, Nick gave the wheels of his chair one powerful shove and covered the distance between them. He wrenched the slipper out of her hand and flung it behind him, his eyes never leaving hers. They were both breathing hard, both menacingly silent as they glared at each other in hostile challenge.

10

"DID I HURT YOU?" Jan asked belligerently. Then, before he could answer, she snapped, "If I did, you deserved it, you distrustful, suspicious-minded worm! It's bad enough to accuse me of such a thing, but to include Allen in your disgusting slander...! Do you have any idea of the hours he put in getting the house ready for you to come home to? Do you even *care* that he's been blaming himself for both your accidents, when it was your own reckless driving that caused the first one and a stupid jackrabbit that caused the second? Damn you, Nick, you don't know what a friend you've got in Allen Whitlow! He's certainly a better friend than you deserve."

By the time she finished the emotional tirade, tears of anger and hurt had left glistening trails down her face. She sniffed loudly and wiped an impatient hand across her cheeks. There was a vulnerable quiver to her mouth, but denunciation blazed from her eyes as more tears spilled out of them. Nick's face was taut and pinched as he impulsively stretched a hand toward her, but she jerked out of his reach with a vehement shake of her head.

"Oh, no," she said. "The other night you told me—no, you *ordered* me not to touch you. Well, now I don't want you touching me."

Nick's head dropped forward. His shoulders slumped, and he lifted a hand to knead the bridge of his nose. She wasn't acting. There wasn't and never had been anything between her and Allen, except friendship. His relief almost equaled the guilt he felt, and the shame. Almost.

"I saw you kiss him last night, out by the pool," he said, not in accusation but as a pathetic attempt at justification. "And this morning, when you took Dolores's things out to his Jeep, the two of you looked so...close."

He slowly lifted his head and appealed to her with his eyes, which were dark and clouded by remorse. Jan felt a tug of compassion, but she held out against it.

"For two days you've been as hateful as you could be to me."

Nick braced himself. His shoulders squared, and he spoke a single word. "Yes."

"I know why." Jan was having trouble keeping her voice steady, but this needed to be said. She had to make him understand that she'd had no other option when she agreed to let Mac operate. "I'm sorry if you feel I betrayed you, Nick, but I'm not sorry for the decision I made. I didn't have any *choice*, dammit!"

A pained look crossed his face, but he didn't look away. "I understand that," he said softly.

"Your mind might understand it, but in your heart you're still blaming me, resenting me," Jan accused bitterly. "Nick—" she lifted a hand in unconscious entreaty, and a fresh crop of tears appeared on her cheeks "—I couldn't risk losing you," she choked out. Though her vision was blurred, she thought he flinched at that. "You'd have done the same thing, if it had been me!"

If I thought you might actually take your own life rather than spend the rest of it in a wheelchair? "Yes. I would have done exactly the same thing."

He spoke so softly, the words barely audible, that Jan thought she hadn't heard right. She stared at him mutely for several seconds, afraid to speak.

"What did you say?" she finally whispered.

"I said...." Nick's voice was rough with emotion, but lacked nothing in conviction as he held her eyes. "I said yes, I'd have done the same thing."

Jan didn't know which of them moved first, and she didn't care. Somehow she got onto his lap and her arms found their way around his neck. She sobbed as if her heart was breaking, when in fact it felt whole again for the first time in almost two months.

"Jan, oh, sweetheart, don't. It's all right, it's all right."

Nick's hoarse murmurs soothed her while his shaking hands stroked her head and back, his touch so tender, so consoling that it set off a fresh bout of weeping. He moaned softly and lifted her face to plant gentle kisses on her streaming eyes, and then her cheeks, and finally her trembling mouth.

As Jan began to respond, they moved toward each other like two ravenous animals, using their mouths and tongues and hands to purge themselves of the fear and uncertainty that had accumulated over the days and weeks. When they finally broke apart they were trembling and panting as if they'd just run a marathon. Jan sagged against Nick's chest in limp exhaustion and heard him suck a ragged breath into his lungs.

"You promised me," he accused in jerky starts and stops, "you'd always remember... that I love you... no matter what."

Jan snuggled closer and wound her arms tight around his neck. "And you promised me," she countered dryly, "that you were going to work on not being such a pain in the—"

"All right, all right!" He looked down at her with a rueful grin. "What say we call it even in the broken-promises department and start over?"

Jan didn't smile, and her eyes were gravely questioning as they searched his. "Can we?"

His grin slipped sideways. "Somewhere between getting hit with my own shoe and the part where you told me how hateful I've been, I realized what a hypocrite I've been. I *would* have done exactly the same thing if our positions had been reversed."

He stopped, and a troubled frown creased his forehead. Jan tenderly soothed it away with cool fingertips. "But..." she prompted gently.

"But...I still feel so damned insecure sometimes, so inadequate," he admitted with gruff reluctance.

Jan shook her head at him. "Nick, think back over the past two and a half days," she said huskily. "How many times have you actually felt 'inadequate'—for any reason? Do you realize you haven't needed help with one single thing?"

Nick's eyes narrowed shrewdly. "If I had, I wouldn't have asked you for it. Which was probably the whole idea, right?" Jan's expression of offended innocence brought a grudging smile to his lips. "Witch," he growled softly. "I had no idea you could be so devious."

"Only when I have to be," Jan told him solemnly. "I figured I was justified in this instance. I wanted back the man I married."

"I'm not the man you married—in the physical sense."

His eyes slid away from hers, and she saw the muscles along his jawline tense. Knowing she must tread delicately, yet also knowing that they had to confront the problem and not pretend it didn't exist,

Jan took her courage in both hands and gently turned his head so that she could look into his eyes.

"You mustn't let it eat at you." Her voice was soft but decisive. "I know it must seem like a long, slow process to you right now, but Mac said—"

Nick stiffened, his eyes flashing resentment. "You talked to Mac about it?"

"No," Jan answered calmly. Her gaze remained steady, unflinching. She refused to back off now that she'd started. "*He* talked to *me*."

There was a pregnant pause, during which she could sense the conflict within him between the desire to know and fear of what the answer might be, before Nick asked hesitantly, "And what did he tell you?"

"That I should be patient and not put any pressure on you. What did he tell *you*?"

Some of the strain disappeared from Nick's face. His mouth quirked wryly. "To be patient and not put any pressure on myself."

"Well, at least he's consistent," Jan murmured with a half smile. "It sounds like good advice."

Nick smiled in agreement, but as he gazed deep into her eyes his amusement was replaced by a much more intense emotion. "God, I love you," he breathed fervently, just before he gathered her to him for a prolonged, breath-stealing kiss. She sensed his need to feel close to her again, to eradicate the anger and pain that had created a wedge between them and regain the special sense of oneness they'd shared before. She let him know, in the way she kissed him back and clung to him, that she felt the same need.

Eventually hunger pangs drove them out of the bungalow and back to the house for lunch. Later that afternoon, they swam together for an hour. Nick had always been a strong swimmer, and he took full advantage of the freedom of movement he enjoyed in the water. The only potentially tense moment came when they decided to leave the pool before they both turned into prunes. Nick had entered the water on his own, without any trouble, but Jan knew he would need help getting out. Should she offer or wait for him to ask? She was reluctant to do either, half afraid he'd react by withdrawing from her again. While she hesitated, Nick glided to her side.

"I think the best way to do this is for you to stay in the water." Turning to put his back against the pool wall, he instructed, "Grab hold behind my knees, and when I start up, give me a good boost."

Jan was so relieved and delighted by his matter-of-fact attitude that she didn't say anything right away. When he was seated on the edge of the pool, she climbed out to push his chair up behind him, steadying it until he was settled, then walked around to kneel in front of him.

"That wasn't so bad, was it?" she asked as she smiled up at him lovingly.

Nick gazed down at the swelling mounds above her bright green bikini bra, and smiled back. "Not bad at all. In fact, I kind of enjoyed it—especially the part when you bent over to take hold of my legs. The view was spectacular."

He hooked a finger in the band of the bra between her breasts, and tugged experimentally. Jan caught his hand and pulled it away with a laugh. "Same old Nick. Can't keep your hands off me, can you?"

"No."

She laughed again at his straight-faced response, then impulsively bent down to plant a kiss on each of his knees, lingering to affectionately rub her cheek against the left one.

"I'm glad. It works both ways, you know." She sat back on her heels, keeping hold of his hand as she gazed up at him earnestly. "The first night you were home...you misunderstood when I touched you. I wasn't just satisfying my curiosity, or 'checking you out,' as you put it," she told him huskily. "I just wanted to feel close to you, to reassure myself that you were really there beside me. I'd really missed having you next to me at night. I wanted to cuddle up next to you. I wanted us to hold each other, maybe fall asleep in each other's arms. I wouldn't have expected anything more. Every night since then, I've had to literally force myself to stay on my side of the bed after you're asleep." She paused to make sure she had his full attention, then added firmly, "But I'm giving you fair warning, Nicholas, tonight we'll both be on *your* side, whether you feel ready for it or not."

Nick bent his head slightly, just enough so that she couldn't read his eyes. He drew a deep, cleansing breath, then exhaled it slowly. "Do you know what I thought, when I got home and saw all the hardware you'd had installed in the house?" he murmured. He looked up, and Jan shook her head mutely.

"I took one look at all the paraphernalia and decided you were making sure you wouldn't *have* to touch me unless it was absolutely necessary. Don't look at me like that, dammit, Jan," he ordered gruffly. "Some women would be repelled by the idea of having physical contact with a man who's paralyzed from the waist down."

"And you lumped me in with those women?" It was more an accusation than a question as she reared back from him. "I ought to hit you for that!"

Surprisingly, Nick's lips twitched in amusement. "If you do, would you hit me here, or here?" He lightly pressed her fingers to his knee and a point about midway up his thigh. "Any higher than that and it could hurt."

Jan yanked her hand away and lifted it to really belt him, and then realized what he was telling her and froze with it in midair. "Nick?" she whispered, and he grinned. *"Nick!"* she repeated in an excited squeal as she threw herself across his legs. She scattered joyful kisses all over his face and neck, until he caught her head in both hands and held her off with an exuberant laugh.

"Good news, huh?"

"Which you've deliberately been keeping from me. As part of the campaign to punish me?" she guessed with an astuteness that made Nick grimace.

"Ouch. You certainly have a way with words."

"But I'm right," Jan insisted, and he heaved a sigh of regret.

"But you're right. And I'm sorry. Forgive?"

"Oh, all right, just this once." Her smile was provocative as she ran her hands down his chest, past his hips to the tops of his thighs. "All the way to here, huh?" she asked in a suggestive murmur.

Nick closed his eyes. His hands settled on top of hers and rotated them slowly, rubbing her palms against the rough warmth of his legs. "Don't get your hopes up," he cautioned in a low, guarded tone. "It's no guarantee."

His misgivings were vindicated later that night. Jan felt his bitter frustration as if it was her own, and the worst part was knowing she had caused it by insisting they try to resume their sexual relationship too soon. She'd done exactly what Mac had warned her not to do.

Nick didn't say anything, but from the way he jabbed at his pillow she suspected it was only because he didn't trust himself to speak.

The next morning she awoke to find him propped over her on an elbow, gazing down at her. He didn't exactly look cheerful, but she couldn't find any sign of resentment or bitterness in his eyes.

"Are you speaking to me?" she asked.

Nick's mouth softened a little. "That depends. What do you want me to say?"

"How about 'good morning,' for a start?" Jan suggested hopefully.

"Good morning for a start. Also, I love you, I'm sorry about last night, and—"

"No!" She hurried to stop him, her eyes full of guilt as she placed a hand over his mouth. "I'm the one who should be sorry, and I am! I was selfish, and inconsiderate, and—"

Nick tugged her hand away in the middle of "inconsiderate," and his mouth landed on hers a second later. "Let's not talk about it, okay?" he asked against her lips. "I'm still feeling a little tender around the old ego. And anyway—" his mouth tilted in a rueful smile "—what I was about to say, before I was so rudely interrupted, was would you please give me a hand getting out of bed? I'm sore as the devil this morning. I think I must have strained every muscle in my body yesterday."

Jan instantly forgot her distress over the debacle she'd caused the night before. Her eyes darkened in concern as she gently laid her palm against his bristly cheek.

"Stella was afraid you might be overdoing it." She rolled out of her side of the bed and came around to Nick's. "Tell me what to do."

"Now that's what I call service," Nick drawled

with a grin. He used the trapeze to sit up, wincing a little. "Get my legs first. Easy! Lord, I can't believe I ache this much."

Jan carefully eased his lower legs off the mattress, then stepped closer to wrap both arms around his waist. While she was so close, she gave him a quick, light kiss, followed by a smile.

Together they swung him from the bed to the chair. The exercise was accompanied by a good bit of theatrical wincing and groaning from Nick, who refused to let her take more of his weight than was absolutely necessary. Jan knelt to place his feet on the footrests while he settled himself more comfortably and released the chair's brake.

"A person would think you'd just been mugged by the entire Rams backfield," she said dryly as she looked up at him. "It can't be *that* bad."

Nick tried on an expression of wounded offense, then abandoned it. "Well, it was worth a try. What does a person have to do to earn a little sympathy around here, anyway—get run over by a Mack truck?"

Jan's mouth fell open. "Sympathy!" she demanded incredulously. "Nick Alexander, the guy who owns the state franchise on stiff-necked male pride, is actually soliciting *sympathy*!"

His grin was a little sheepish. "Yeah, well...all things considered, my pride seems to be in fairly decent shape this morning. Anyway, I wouldn't exactly spit in your eye if you wanted to fuss over me a little bit."

Jan's eyes were luminous with love as she rose to her feet. She moved to his side and tenderly wrapped her arms around his shoulders, cradling his head against her. "Sorry, Ace, but I'm fresh out of sympathy," she murmured huskily. "Would you settle for heaps and gobs of good old-fashioned TLC?''

Nick's arms slipped around her waist, and he burrowed his face into the warm valley between her breasts. ''Sounds like just what the doctor ordered,'' he answered in a muffled voice. ''But, Jan?''

She stroked his bare back lovingly. ''Hmm?''

''Could we delay the first dose for a few minutes? I really do have to get to the bathroom.''

She chuckled as she bent to kiss his tousled hair, then pulled away and gave his chair a solid shove toward the bathroom door. ''Your breakfast'll be ready in fifteen minutes.''

Nick paused to glance back over his shoulder. ''It takes me longer than that just to get dressed,'' he protested.

''So don't bother to get dressed,'' Jan retorted. One eyelid lowered in a flirtatious wink before she strolled out of the room.

Nick's good spirits were still in evidence when Stella arrived. While the two of them were occupied in the bungalow, Jan impulsively placed a call to Mac. After reporting on Nick's progress, she asked a couple of concise questions, the answers to which improved her already-optimistic mood. When Stella came back through the house to collect her purse and sunglasses, Jan quizzed her casually about whether Nick might expect to experience a repeat of that morning's muscle soreness.

''I doubt it,'' Stella replied. ''He worked most of the kinks out today, in addition to which I gave him a pretty vigorous massage. He's really in fantastic shape, you know—his overall muscle tone's terrific. If he does stiffen up a little, it'll probably be in the upper back and shoulders, and a good back rub should take care of it.'' She grinned suggestively.

"Of course if that good-lookin' devil was mine, I'd rub his back whether it needed it or not. A nice long massage often stimulates more than just the circulation, know what I mean?"

As Jan closed the front door behind Stella, she was smiling. *Oh, yes, Stel, I certainly do know what you mean, and by this time tomorrow so will that good-lookin' devil I'm married to.* She had received encouraging advice from two knowledgeable sources today, and she fully intended to make the best possible use of it.

After lunch Nick went straight out to the pool. Jan washed the dishes and started a load of laundry before joining him. When she came out of the house she was surprised to find him not in the water but stretched out on a chaise, apparently contemplating the vivid blue of the sky. His hands were linked behind his head and there was an expression of deep concentration in his eyes.

"Why aren't you swimming laps?" she asked as she perched on the edge of the chaise.

Her voice seemed to pull him back from wherever he'd been. "Mmm? Oh, I decided to soak up some rays first. You know, I'd forgotten how good the sun feels on a day like this, or a puff of breeze against your skin. We tend to take the simple things for granted, don't we?"

Jan reached out to stroke an unruly lock of hair off his forehead. "I suppose we do, most of the time," she agreed pensively. "Until something happens to shake us up, make us realize what we've been looking at without seeing."

"Or how blessed we are," Nick murmured, lifting his eyes to hers. He smiled, and Jan suddenly longed to throw herself down beside him and twine around his body like a vine. The urge wasn't motivated by sexual desire, but rather the simple, uncomplicated wish to be close to him, feel the warmth of his body against hers. She unconsciously leaned closer, her eyes soft and yearning.

"Well?" Nick coaxed softly as he held out an arm in invitation. "Come on, woman. You're about to fall on me, anyway."

She needed no further persuasion. She nestled against him eagerly, her arm draping across his waist as her head settled onto his shoulder. "I didn't want you to feel pressured," she murmured with a blissful sigh.

"Rest easy. I don't."

"Just loved," she added, snuggling still closer.

"Just loved," Nick concurred huskily. He pressed a kiss on the top of her head. "You do a jim-dandy job of making me feel loved, even when I know good and well I don't deserve to be."

His voice was rich and warm, as caressing as his hand, which was traveling lazily up and down the arm resting on his torso. On the next downward pass, he clasped her wrist, moving her hand from his waist to the top of his leg, just below his navy swim trunks. Jan's pulse fluttered, and she cautiously administered a gentle squeeze.

"Mmm, that felt good," Nick sighed into her hair. "You know, it's crazy, but I feel better—about everything—today than I have in I don't know how long."

"I can tell," Jan said, a smile in her voice. "It's good to see you so relaxed. You're positively mellow." He gave her a brief squeeze in response, and she turned her head fractionally to kiss his collarbone. "What exactly were you thinking about when I came outside?"

"I've had an idea for a new book. Don't ask what it's about," he warned before she could. "So far it's

just the germ of an idea, and you know how super-
stitious I am at that stage. If it develops into anything, you'll be the first to know."

Jan subdued her curiosity, but not her elation.
Throwing himself into a new book would be the best
possible thing he could do now. While Stella and
time saw to the recovery of his body, a book to work
on would provide therapy for his emotions, keep his
mind too occupied to allow impatience or frustration to set in.

After dinner he went into his office to store a few
random thoughts in the word processor while they
were still fresh, he told Jan. More than two hours
later she peeked in to find him still at the keyboard,
totally absorbed.

"Nick?"

"Not now. Go away," he muttered absently, not
even shifting his eyes from the monitor.

"But it's after ten. You've been at it for hours!"

"Scram!" The command was an ominous growl,
and Jan grinned happily as she backed out the door
without another word. He might well stay holed up
in there for another two or three hours, and she could
put the time to good use by catching a little sleep.

Jan half woke when he came to bed, turning toward him with a mumbled question. She was wriggling up against him before he was quite settled, and
she instinctively reached out to put both arms
around him and help shift his body until he was
comfortable.

As Nick gazed down at the seal-dark head resting
so sweetly on his chest, a lump the size of a golf ball
formed in his throat. Even in sleep she molded herself to him so perfectly, as if she was the other half of
him. He loved her so much at that moment he could
hardly bear it. His eyes misted over, and something

inside his chest swelled until he felt the pressure in his throat. He longed to stroke her body out of its supple, relaxed slumber, feel her beneath his hands and mouth as he aroused her.

His fingers moved restlessly against her skin. If he did wake her.... His heart speeded up, his mouth went dry. If he did, would he be able to—

Ruthlessly cutting off the rest of the thought, he willed his mind to empty, until sleep finally stole in to fill the void.

In his fevered dream he made love to her like a lust-crazed animal, driving into her again and again, tirelessly, losing himself in her, finding himself in her. But gradually, almost imperceptibly at first, the dream began to change. He was more gentle, now, loving her tenderly, slowly, and she was so warm, so soft, so welcoming. His lashes fluttered against his cheeks, and then his eyes were fully open, and dream had suddenly become reality.

"Oh, God!"

When she heard his choked cry, Jan's free hand glided over his stomach and up his chest, where it was seized and gripped with crushing strength.

"Jan, oh, Jan!"

She lifted her head to look at him. Her long, inky hair trailed over his leg as she raised herself. She smiled into his eyes, which were like green flames in the dark, and gracefully swung one slender leg over him to kneel astride his hips.

Nick moaned as he watched her straddle him. She was still wearing that soft, loving smile and nothing else. Though he saw her and felt her fingers still curled firmly around him, he was half convinced this wasn't really happening, that he was still dreaming. And then she lowered herself to take him inside her, and a low moan escaped him. This was no dream.

Their hands began to caress in unison, stoking the fires. She rubbed her palms over his arms, traced intricate designs on his chest and belly with her fingertips, explored the ridges of his pelvis, teased the sensitive skin of his inner thighs. His hands shaped the firm contours of her buttocks, squeezing lightly, then moved up, skating over the curve of her waist and onto her leanly fleshed ribs, finally reaching her breasts, worshiping them with a gentle care that made her gasp with pleasure.

She felt the tension build in him as he guided her, knew the exact instant when his control broke. A triumphant smile flickered across her face as his grip abruptly tightened.

"Oh, Jan, it's been so long. I'm sorry, baby, but I can't wait—"

"It's all right," she told him in a husky murmur. Bracing her arms on his chest, she leaned down to kiss him. "This time's for you." From somewhere she summoned the strength to increase their rhythm, knowing she was driving him past the point of no return and glorying in the knowledge. Joy spiraled through her when she heard his deep, tortured groan and felt his muscles clench.

Nick tried to hold off his climax, not sure he'd stay hard long enough to bring Jan to hers. But when she told him softly, "This time's for you," he knew he was lost. He was deaf to her murmured words of encouragement as a series of uncontrollable explosions ripped through him, rocketing him over the edge of sanity and hurling him toward the heavens. His mind had barely started to clear before he began directing her movements again, and her flight into oblivion followed his almost immediately. Grateful relief washed through him when she cried his name at the end, her voice filled with ecstatic joy and love, her hands gripping his shoulders so hard that her nails scratched the skin.

Jan swayed, and as she toppled forward his arms were there to catch her and hold her close to his heaving chest. They were both gasping, both wonderfully exhausted.

"I didn't think— How did you know?" Nick asked when he could speak.

Jan sighed, arranging herself squarely on top of him. "Mac. I called him today. He clued me in on a couple of interesting facts about the physiology of the healthy adult male body." Rubbing her cheek against his chest with a smile, she elaborated. "He said I *should* 'check you out' when you were unaware of it, preferably in the middle of the night while you were in deep sleep, and go from there. Devious, conniving soul that I am, I was only too willing to follow his suggestion. Worked out pretty well, didn't it?"

Nick's arms contracted in a fierce hug as he buried his face in her throat. His voice was gravelly with emotion. "Healthy adult male body, huh?"

"*Very* healthy, as I can personally attest. Extraordinarily, *fab*ulously healthy. Any healthier and I'd be in a coma."

Nick hugged her again, feeling so full of love he thought he might choke. "Remind me to pay Mac's bill," he muttered thickly. "And maybe throw in a little something extra."

Jan smiled as her arms wound around his neck. "Can I stay like this for a while?" she mumbled drowsily.

"Please. All damned night."

"Mmm, you talked me into it." She yawned and squirmed against him in a sleepy stretch. "I'm bushed. I've been awake since midnight."

Nick turned his head to look at the digital clock beside the bed. It read 3:26. He placed a gentle kiss on her forehead and felt her warm breath fan his chest as she drifted off to sleep.

THE NEXT MORNING both he and Jan overslept. Neither of them had remembered to set the alarm, and it was almost nine when Jan shook him awake. With Stella due to arrive at any minute, his hopes for a morning devoted to leisurely lovemaking had to be shelved. Then there was his own frustrating inability to get ready quickly.

The morning rapidly went from bad to worse. His therapy session was a disaster from beginning to end. First his hand slipped while he was pulling himself onto the exercise table and he fell heavily, banging his elbow in the process. Then, after Stella had half lifted him back onto the table, which was humiliating enough in itself, she insisted on trying a new series of exercises that were utterly impossible for him to execute. By the time she left, his morale was at its lowest point in days, and he was simmering with frustration and rage.

He entered the house and went to the kitchen for a glass of water while Jan saw Stella to the door. She always left a few glasses on the counter for him to use, but for some reason this morning there were none to be seen. Her oversight was the last straw. Dammit, what was he supposed to do, sit and wait for his wife to come and get a glass for him, as if he were a helpless cripple?

Setting his jaw grimly, he twisted at the waist and laid both forearms on the smooth Formica counter top. Levering himself up out of the chair was a cinch, and he even managed to open the cabinet door and retrieve a glass from the shelf. It was when he started to lower himself into the chair again, feeling rather smug about his success, that disaster struck. He realized too late that he'd neglected to set the brake.

"Hell and damnation," he muttered as the chair started to roll backward across the waxed hardwood floor. He fell awkwardly, cracking his elbow again and landing on his side with his face pressed against the baseboard cabinets.

"Nick! Are you all right?"

At the sound of Jan's anxious voice, he heaved over onto his back, wincing as he raised up. That she should have seen him fall was the final indignity. He lashed out at her before she'd covered half the distance from the door.

"No, I'm damn well not all right!" he snarled. Jan halted, her concern changing to shock as he raged on. "I can't move so much as my big toe. I have to drag myself into a wheelchair every morning and out of it every night, and I can't function sexually unless my wife takes me by surprise while I'm in the middle of an erotic dream. Dammit, Jan," he muttered heavily, the worst of his anger spent, "I know I said I'd stopped resenting you for it, but right now I feel so damned angry that I'm in this mess...."

He didn't look directly into her face until he finished. What he saw instantly jolted him out of his self-involvement. She looked stricken, her lovely eyes filled with a disillusioned hurt that no amount of tears would alleviate. Still they fell, trickling silently down her face as she stood stock-still in the middle of the room. As he watched in shaken, confused silence, her mouth quivered pitifully. Then she turned and walked out the door without a word.

It took several minutes for him to scoot across the room and hoist himself back into the chair, by which time he had given himself a good going-over for taking his frustration out on Jan. She'd lavished him with loving support and encouragement for two months, and he'd paid her back by behaving like a spoiled, ungrateful child.

When he entered the living room he noticed that the sliding patio door was open. Thinking she might have gone out to the bungalow, he rolled down the ramp and started toward it. He was about halfway across the patio when he saw her. She was in the horse lot, which abutted her garden. He called to her, but she ignored him. When he reached the edge of the patio, he stopped. He'd have a devil of a time trying to propel his chair over the lawn and the bare, uneven strip of dirt beyond it.

"Jan," he called again. "Come back to the house, please. I'm sorry I lost my temper just now."

Jan tuned out the sound of his coaxing voice. Her tears had dried, but there was a tightness in her throat that told her it wouldn't take much to start her crying again. When Sandy saw her, he nickered softly and came to nuzzle her chest in greeting. She gave his neck an affectionate pat, then slipped the bridle on and stepped to his side to mount.

"Jan!"

From the corner of her eye she saw Nick leave the patio and start pushing his chair across the lawn. The one thing she couldn't do at the moment was face him, at least not with any semblance of composure. Grasping the reins and Sandy's mane in her left hand, she placed the right on his bare back, ready to jump up and pull herself astride.

"Jan! What do you think you're doing, for pete's sake—he hasn't been ridden in more than two months." Now a note of anxiety had entered Nick's voice.

Her lips compressed stubbornly as she hopped aboard the big gelding. *Don't listen.*

"Don't go off like this, honey, please. Come back and give me a chance—"

Don't listen!

Nick wrestled the chair over the strip of land separating the lawn from the horse lot, cursing silently. He damned the rough, cracked ground, the suddenly unwieldy chair and his own useless legs, which wouldn't let him get up and run to stop her. His voice held angry desperation as he tried one more time.

"*Jan! Please!*"

If he didn't know better, he'd have sworn she hadn't even heard him. She leaned down to open the gate at the far side of the lot and rode through it, while he was still floundering six feet short of the near fence.

JAN GRIMACED as she plopped down on a rock to shake a tablespoonful of grit out of her tennis shoe. By now Sandy was no doubt at home wolfing down his lunch, unknowing and uncaring that she was still at least two miles from the house. Darn that horse, anyway! She'd dismounted for a few minutes to sit and contemplate her future, and he'd run off and left her stranded a good seven or eight miles from home.

At least the walk back had given her plenty of time to think. She'd reached a hard decision as she tramped along, one she knew was going to be as painful to act on as it had been to make. She was going to leave Nick. Not permanently—at least, she hoped not—but until he'd rid himself of his resentment toward her. It was the only thing she could do. She couldn't go on like this, up one minute and down the next, never knowing when the resentment might flare up again and cause him to attack her as he had that morning.

Maybe if she wasn't around to constantly remind him of her "betrayal," his bitterness would start to fade, especially once he was on his feet again. When he was fully recovered he'd surely be able to regain his objectivity.

Sighing wearily, she retied her shoe and started walking again. She'd thought it all out, even to where she would go when she left. Not to her parents', that was for sure. They wouldn't understand, and they'd probably pressure her to return to Nick at once. She had an old friend from college who lived in Albuquerque, and they'd stayed in fairly regular contact during the past three years. Of course there were other friends scattered all over the country, but she couldn't bring herself to put *too* much distance between herself and Nick. At least if she went to Albuquerque, she'd know they were still in the same state.

The worst part was going to be actually leaving. Nick would make a scene, she just knew he would, and she was afraid she might not be able to stick to her decision if he really tried to convince her not to leave. Somehow she had to, though. For the sake of her own pride, which at the moment had to be at least as battered as his, she had to separate from him for a while. So far she'd gone all the way for him, and then some. Now it was his turn. Either he loved her enough to set aside his stupid resentment, or he didn't. And oh, what would she do if the gamble she was taking didn't pay off?

NICK HAD ALREADY BEEN WORRYING for close to two hours when Jan's horse returned without her. Though he couldn't get close enough to inspect the animal, there didn't seem to be a mark on him—no blood, no scratches or any other sign that he'd been in an accident. The big buckskin trotted happily through the open gate and made straight for his feed and then his water.

"Where the hell is she?" Nick demanded of the horse as he shoved his chair up to the fence. Sandy raised his head to blow him a raspberry, then calmly returned his attention to his meal.

"If you've thrown her, you big ugly brute, if she's hurt I'll see your carcass turned into dog food."

The assurance was given in a low, throbbing voice before Nick impatiently turned his chair around to head back for the house. Five minutes later Allen's Jeep swerved into the driveway and screeched to a halt. Nick was already rolling down the ramp as Allen jumped out. "Thanks for coming." He grinned shakily.

"How long has she been gone?" Allen demanded.

"A couple of hours. Allen, if anything's happened to her—"

"No!" Allen cut in sharply as he hurried around the front of the Jeep. "Don't even think it. She's an expert rider—you know that."

Nick responded in a tense snarl. "If she's such an expert rider, how did her horse manage to come back without her? Come on, dammit, get me up in this thing so we can start looking for her."

The fact that Allen had to lift him into the Jeep didn't faze him. All he felt was impatience to get started, and an irrational, unnerving anxiety. Though he was trying hard not to acknowledge it, he had a deep-down feeling that something was terribly wrong, that this day was destined to end even more badly than it had begun.

As Allen reversed out of the drive, Sandy lifted his head toward the west and whinnied softly. A few minutes later Jan trudged up to the gate, closed and secured it and leaned against it to glare at him.

"Thanks a heap, pal," she muttered, removing Sandy's bridle. "Another stunt like that and you'll be on your way to the glue factory."

As she headed for the house the horse whinnied again, as if to protest the appalling threats that had been made against him that day.

WHEN THE JEEP PULLED INTO THE DRIVE, Nick immediately noticed that the garage door was open, the Mustang gone.

"Thank God," he murmured fervently. "She's been here and left again."

His relief was short-lived. The first thing he saw when they entered the house was a white envelope propped on the library table just inside the front door. His name was on it, written in Jan's precise script. He picked it up, but once he had it in his hand he suddenly didn't want to open it.

"Probably a note telling you she's gone to town for groceries or something," Allen said from behind him. He didn't sound convinced, though.

Nick held the envelope as if he expected it to explode in his hand. "Yeah, probably. Listen, how about some coffee—or better yet, a beer. Chasing around in this heat all afternoon really dried me out."

"Aren't you going to open it?" Allen asked quietly as he tagged along to the kitchen.

Nick didn't answer until he'd taken two beers from the fridge and passed one to Allen. "To tell the truth, I think I'm afraid to."

He said it so calmly that the words didn't register

right away. When they did, Allen frowned down at the bottle in his hand, worrying his lower lip with his teeth. He lifted his eyes to Nick, and the other man's grim expression helped him make up his mind. Still, he took a fortifying swig from the bottle first.

"We need to talk," he said, and the gravity in his voice caught Nick's full attention.

What Allen had to say didn't take long. When he'd finished, Nick stared at him as if he'd just rattled off the secret to eternal life.

"You're sure?" he asked, his voice a little hoarse. "You're absolutely sure? Mac expects me out of this chair within two months? Why didn't anyone tell me?"

"We didn't want you to feel any pressure to make a deadline." Allen set his bottle on the counter with a disgusted oath. "I could kick myself for not saying something to you sooner. I suspected you'd think the worst when you saw all the—"

"Hardware," Nick furnished dryly. He covered his face with both hands, his fingers pressing into his eye sockets. "Don't blame yourself, for pity's sake. I should have known she wouldn't lie to me...." His voice trailed off and he dropped his hands. "But she said she knew I felt betrayed, and why. What was she talking about?"

"I can answer that," Allen said. "It was because you'd made it clear you'd never willingly submit to surgery. She figured you'd hold it against her for signing the consent forms."

Nick gaped at him in astonished disbelief. "That's crazy! I'd have *died* if she hadn't signed those forms! You can't mean to tell me that all this time she thought I was resenting her for *that*?"

Allen nodded solemnly. His eyes dropped to the

envelope in Nick's lap. "I think you'd better open that." He hesitated, then added in an almost pitying voice, "I'll be at home if you...need anything."

Nick heard the front door close as he tore open the envelope. As his eyes scanned the single sheet of paper inside, his fingers clenched and the blood drained from his face. He made himself read it twice more, praying each time that the words would change.

"No," he said in a ragged whisper when his mind finally had to accept what his heart was still denying. "Dammit to hell, *no*!"

JAN LET HERSELF INTO THE FURNISHED APARTMENT and slipped out of her shoes with a sigh of relief. Today's assignment had been exhausting, and she was really looking forward to a long hot shower and then maybe a bowl of soup and a salad—something light for supper.

Her friend Megan had been a doll to recommend this place to her, and her to the landlady. The apartment was actually the top half of Mrs. Brody's house, and she was particular about who she allowed to rent the place. It was ideal for Jan's needs: small, cozy and hard to find.

The lengths to which she'd gone to frustrate any efforts at tracking her down had been a little ridiculous, she had to admit. She felt like the heroine in one of Nick's books—running, hiding out, using a phony name. Well, it wasn't actually *phony*; she'd "borrowed" her mother's maiden name, and for the time being she was Janet Weaver. Of course her mother didn't know that. Jan was convinced that if anyone managed to trace her to Albuquerque, it would be Dolores, and she had taken some pretty extraordinary steps to prevent that from happening.

After her shower and supper, she curled up on Mrs. Brody's chintz-covered sofa and made one of her thrice-weekly long-distance calls. Dolores answered on the second ring.

"Hi, it's your loving daughter."

"I don't have a daughter."

Jan sighed. "Please, mother, it's been a long day."

"Have you called Nick yet?"

"No. Do we really have to go over this again?" Then, not giving Dolores a chance to respond, she asked, "Have *you* talked to him lately?"

"You know very well that he calls here four or five times a week, Janet Faye. I speak to him more often than I speak to you, and I must say the conversations with my son-in-law are much more enjoyable than the ones with my daughter."

"Hey, give me a break," Jan complained. "I write you a couple of times a week, too."

Dolores made a noise that sounded like a harrumph. "And your letters are always so interesting."

Jan grinned. "You mean the postmarks are."

"Don't be smart with your mother, Janet. By the way, where can I expect my next letter to come from?"

"Houston."

"Hmm, that would be Karen Stanton. Don't you think you're overdoing it a bit? I mean, really, Janet—sending my letters all over the country for your friends to mail for you! It's like something out of a bad spy movie. Lord knows what they all think, and it's beginning to get a bit tiresome."

"Mother, if I didn't do it this way we both know you'd track me down like a bloodhound, and then come after me and try to drag me back to my husband, whether I wanted to go or not."

"Are you telling me you *don't* want to go back to him?" Dolores demanded sharply.

"No! Of course not!" Jan's voice softened, became wistful. "I miss him like crazy. How is he?"

"Call him and ask him that yourself."

"Oh, mother." Jan paused a moment, rubbing her fingers over her forehead. "At least tell me if he's walking yet, on his own. If I just knew that much—"

"Do you know how that sounds, Janet?" Dolores cut in shortly. "It sounds like you'll only go back to him if and when he's completely able-bodied again—like you don't want a husband who's confined to a wheelchair."

"Mother!" Jan was appalled. "How can you say a thing like that? You know that's not true!"

"I don't know anything," Dolores snapped in exasperation. "You refuse to *tell* me anything, and Nick isn't much more enlightening. If I didn't love you both so much, and truly believe that you belong together, I swear I'd wash my hands of the two of you." Her voice warming a little, she urged, "At least call him, Janet. He's hurting."

"So am I, mother," Jan murmured. "So am I. And I will go back, just as soon as I know he's on his feet again. I thought he would be by now. It's been almost three months since I left." Gnawing on her lower lip, she mumbled, "Mac *promised* me... he was certain Nick would be walking again in a couple of months."

"Yes, well, he wasn't counting on the fact that you'd abandon Nick in the middle of his convalescence, was he?" Dolores sniped. "I'd think the emotional strain alone would be enough to set his recovery back. The mind can play some pretty dirty tricks on the body, you know, Janet," she added slyly. "Maybe he won't be *able* to walk again until and unless his runaway wife comes back to him."

"That sounds pretty farfetched, mother," Jan scoffed, but there was a trace of uncertainty in her voice she wasn't aware of, and her teeth returned to nibble at her lip again.

"You're probably right," Dolores murmured, her tone mild. "I'm no expert, heaven knows. Oh, I almost forgot—Nick did mention something that should interest you, the last time he called."

Jan pounced just as her mother had intended. "What? What is it?" she demanded, hungry for any bit of news from him, no matter how small.

"You won't like it," Dolores warned, and Jan's heart thumped against her ribs.

"Mother! Tell me!"

"He's hired a private investigator to find you."

Jan's mouth opened on a gasp. That had been the last thing she'd expected to hear. She didn't know whether she was dismayed or pleased.

"Janet? Are you still there?" Dolores's impatient voice demanded in her ear.

"Yes. I don't think it'll do him any good, mother. I've been careful to cover my tracks."

"But you told me you were working. If you have a job, there must be records of some kind, and you surely had to give references."

Dolores sounded so smug that Jan smiled. "I hate to disappoint you, mother, but I'm not using my own name," she said dryly.

"Why, that's . . . that's . . ." Dolores sputtered.

"Very clever, I know. And I only needed one reference, as it happens—the friend who recommended me for the job. She works at the same place."

Dolores tried another tack. "What exactly are you doing, anyway? You never did say."

"I know I didn't," Jan replied wryly. "But I guess

it wouldn't hurt to tell you. I'm working as a staff photographer for a Sunday supplement. Heaven knows why, but when I left I decided at the last minute to take along my photographic equipment. As it turned out, I'm glad I did. I also hired two college students to take Nick's car back the day after I got here," she added with a mischievous grin. "I gave them a map, and told them to park it in the garage between nine and ten-thirty in the morning, when I knew he'd be out in the bungalow. So this private eye he's hired won't be able to trace me through the license plate or registration. I covered my tracks really well."

"You've been watching too many detective shows on television," Dolores muttered. "Why does everything always have to be so complicated with you? Would you believe that some of my friends actually have daughters who live with their husbands? Some of them even have a grandchild or two to dote on. But not me. Oh, no, *my* daughter thinks she's an undercover agent in one of her husband's novels. Go home, Janet. Straighten out this mess with Nick, whatever it is, so we can all go back to living like normal people. I'm too old for all this complicated intrigue."

Jan's smile was a bit rueful as she laid her hand on the bulge below her waistline. "Soon, mother, I promise," she murmured. "There is one small complication you don't even know about, but I think this one will ultimately turn out to have a positive effect for all of us."

LATER THAT NIGHT, Dolores received another long-distance call.

"Well, any news?"

"Don't be so abrupt, Nick. How are you? Still stiff and sore?"

"No, that was only temporary. I'm fine. Did she call today?"

"Yes, just a little while ago. Are you still using the cane?"

"Hell, no, I got rid of that last week. Dolores, for pity's sake!"

"All right, all right. Sometimes I wonder how Janet put up with you as long as she did."

"Dolores!" Her name was a menacing growl.

"Calm down, Nick," his mother-in-law instructed placidly. "Now, what do you want first—a report on Jan's call, or the information Evan's friend at the phone company came up with?"

Nick gave an excited whoop. "He traced her calls? You've actually got a number? Hold on, let me get this down. Okay, shoot."

"By the way, I told her you'd hired a private investigator to find her."

"You *what*?"

"I thought it might shake her up a little. I also hinted that being so cruelly abandoned might have adversely affected your recovery. That *really* got to her, I could tell."

"Lord have mercy," Nick breathed in awe. "Now I know where she got that devious mind. You're really enjoying this, aren't you?"

Dolores's smile came through over the line. "As a matter of fact, I am, rather. Now, here's the number. It's in Albuquerque."

THE NEXT MORNING Ma Bell's lines were humming again. This time Jan called Allen.

"*Jan!*" he blurted when she'd identified herself. He turned startled, questioning eyes on Nick, who was lounging on his sofa as he sipped a can of beer. Nick made a slashing gesture with one hand and shook his head as he sat forward. "Uh, well, this is certainly a surprise! How are you? Worried?" Allen repeated, his brows shooting toward his hairline. "About Nick?"

Nick sank back against the sofa cushions with a pleased smile. Allen flashed him a wicked, conspiratorial grin.

"Well, I don't really think it's my place to discuss his physical condition with you," he said in his most reserved, professional tone. "All I can say is that he seems to be doing as well as can be expected." That brought Nick upright again as he choked on his beer. "Oh, hell! Sorry, Jan, I've gotta go. Dawg's after one of the chickens."

"Nice touch," Nick commented dryly after Allen dropped the receiver back in its cradle. "I hope I survive long enough to drive to Albuquerque."

Allen chuckled and rubbed his palms together. "Have you got the address yet?"

"No. The friend who's checking it out said he should have it by this afternoon. I figured I'd hit the road first thing in the morning. If I don't catch her at home, I'll go straight to the newspaper office." He grinned. "Can you imagine the look on her face when I saunter up to her desk and tell her to collect her stuff?"

Allen winced. "You know, in a way this is kind of mean. I think I may board up my doors and windows tonight. There's no telling how she'll react when she finds out you've had everybody conspiring against her, including her own mother."

Nick rose easily to his feet. He sighed, then gave a fatalistic shrug. "I'll just point out that she would have done exactly the same thing," he said with a crooked smile. "I'd better get home, in case Hal calls with the address." At the door, he paused to look back. "Do me a favor, will you—make yourself scarce for a few days. Your neighbors have a honeymoon to finish."

12

JAN TURNED THE RENTED CAR into the driveway and braked to a stop in front of the garage door. She sat for a minute, fighting the urge to turn around and drive back to Albuquerque. She knew that if she did, she would only end up coming back again. She had to see him for herself, make sure he was all right. She refused to speculate about what would happen after that.

Slowly she got out of the car, rubbing her damp palms over the legs of her maternity slacks. She glanced down at the obvious evidence of her pregnancy. How would he react to that little surprise? *Please, let him be happy,* she prayed silently as she walked to the front door. She was so nervous that she failed to notice the ramp had been removed.

The door was unlocked. She slipped inside as if she were a thief and hesitantly crept across the entry.

"Nick?" Her voice was little more than a hoarse whisper. There was no answer. She cleared her throat and called again. "Nick? Are you in the house?"

She turned toward the hall just as the patio door slid open. The sound alerted her, and she froze.

"Jan? *Jan!*"

She closed her eyes and took a deep breath before turning to face him. He'd obviously been in the pool. His hair was mussed where he'd rubbed it with the towel hanging around his neck, and drops of water glistened on his shoulders and in the hair of his chest. He absently shoved the door shut with one hand, his face pale as his astonished gaze dropped to her stomach. He took two halting steps forward.

"Jan!"

She swayed as the floor seemed to tilt beneath her. "You're dripping water all over the rug," she said in a dazed voice, and then she fainted for the second time in her life.

When she opened her eyes Nick's face filled her vision, his eyes darkened by anxiety. She was lying on the sofa. He was kneeling on the floor at her side.

"What— How did I get over here?" she asked in confusion. She started to sit up, but Nick's hand on her shoulder held her down.

"No, stay there! I carried you. Are you all right?" The sentences were clipped, his voice taut and strained.

Jan frowned. "Of course I'm all right. It was just a shock, seeing you—" A gasp cut off the rest as she remembered and her hand flew over her mouth. "Oh! Oh, Nick!" she cried as tears spurted to her eyes. "You were standing up—and walking! I saw you!"

Her arms flew open, and Nick filled them at once as he leaned over her, holding her with fierce gentleness while she wept with joy.

"Oh, I was so worried," she wailed. "I thought something had g-gone wr-wrong, and I— Oh, hold me, please hold me. I'm so h-h-happy!"

Nick made a sound into her hair that was part laugh and part sob. "I never would have guessed. Lord, you scared me! I just barely caught you before you hit the floor. Promise you won't make a habit of that; I don't think my heart could take it."

Jan laughed through her tears and tightened her hold on his neck. "Nick, Nick! You can walk!" she said ecstatically.

He pulled back to smile down at her. "And run, and hop, skip and jump. And chase after you if you ever decide to pull your little disappearing act again."

Jan shook her head adamantly. "I won't," she promised in a husky voice. "I wouldn't have this time, but I just couldn't stay, knowing you were resenting me—"

"You were wrong," Nick interrupted softly. "At least, you were wrong about the *reason* I was such a jerk. Darling, I *never* felt any resentment about the surgery. How could I? Did you honestly think I'd have wanted you to let me die?"

"You said you would have," Jan murmured uncertainly, and he winced.

"Don't remind me. When I think of what I put you through—what I put us both through—" He heaved a disgusted sigh. "All I can say is that I'm sorry for being such a royal pain, and incredibly stupid on top of it. But most of all I'm sorry for driving you away." His voice deepened and became harsh. "God, I've missed you."

"I've missed you, too," Jan murmured tearfully as he gathered her close and pressed his face to her neck. "So much, so much."

They moved at the same time, their mouths meeting in joyous reunion. After a while Nick pulled away a little to string urgent kisses over her face. His hands became restless, and he murmured increasingly erotic love words between kisses. Jan giggled happily. But when one of his caressing hands strayed to what had formerly been her flat tummy, he jumped back as if he'd been scalded.

"Omigod!" he croaked. "I forgot. How could I have forgotten? Jan—you're *pregnant*!"

He sounded so astonished that she laughed. "*We're* pregnant, Mr. Alexander. Almost five months. Isn't it terrific?"

Nick shook his head dazedly. There was a look approaching reverence on his face as he reached out to cautiously lay his hand on her distended midsection.

"A baby," he breathed in wonder. "That's our baby in there." He swallowed hard. "Oh, Jan, Jan."

When he bent to rest his cheek beside his hand, Jan closed her eyes against a surging wave of love more powerful than anything she'd ever known. And then she felt him gently move her clothes aside so that he could press a soft kiss on her skin, and a sob of pure joy jerked against her throat.

"Come up here, daddy," she asked in a husky voice.

Nick lifted his head. His smile was a little wobbly, and there was an unnatural brightness to his eyes. "Sure there's room for the three of us?"

She held out her arms to him, squirming against the back of the sofa as he came up beside her. They lay face to face, arms around each other. Nick applied gentle pressure to the small of her back so that her stomach pressed against him and rested his forehead on hers.

"This is really stupid," Jan blubbered. "Why am I crying? Why are *you* crying?"

Nick smiled and used a corner of the towel to pat at her eyes and cheeks. Jan smiled back and followed his example with the other end. "There's nothing stupid about it," he said firmly. "We're pregnant, and pregnant people are supposed to be emotional. It's one of the rules."

"You know everything. You're going to be one terrific daddy."

"Oh, I hope so," Nick whispered, and the emotion in his voice brought still more tears to her eyes. He kissed her, his lips soft and loving. "But for the time being, I'd like to practice being a terrific husband. Do you have any idea how sexually exciting your round little tummy is, or how aroused I am?"

Jan grinned. "No, I can't say that I'd noticed."

"Come on," Nick growled, "you're not that big yet."

"Neither are you, apparently."

His head jerked back as a surprised laugh escaped him. He pulled one of her hands between them, pressing it hard against the bulge at the front of his trunks. "Care to revise your opinion?"

"Well—" she grinned smugly "—we'll have to find a way to solve your...predicament."

"Can we? Is it safe?" Even as he asked, Nick was tugging at her slacks, easing them over her hips. "It won't hurt you or the baby?"

"Neither of us. Oh, Nick, I want you so much, *need* you so much! Do you realize how long it's been?"

"To the minute." He moved, quickly and deftly dispensing with their remaining clothes. When he returned to lay his naked body along hers, he asked hoarsely, "Tell me again, and keep on telling me."

She tried, but it was hard to talk and gasp and whimper and moan all at the same time, so she just concentrated on showing him. He didn't seem to mind. They lay tangled together for a while, spent and thoroughly satisfied. Nick nuzzled her neck affectionately, then slid down to lightly kiss her stomach.

"Just so Dawg, Jr., doesn't feel completely left

out," he said with a grin. "Stay right there for a minute. I've got a couple of surprises for you."

He sprang to his feet with an easy grace that thrilled Jan, then disappeared down the hall. When he returned, he was carrying a box. A large manila envelope rested on top of it. Jan sat up in excitement. The box was exactly the right size to hold a book manuscript. Nick placed the two items on the end of the sofa, then sat beside her and pulled her across his lap.

"This one first." He handed her the box.

Jan lifted the lid and laid it aside. Nick was silent as she read the title page: *Winners* by Nick Alexander.

"This is the one I started the day before you left," he said softly. "I finished it while you were gone. Read the dedication."

Jan removed the title page to see the page beneath it. Tears misted her eyes, and she blinked to clear them as she read aloud, "'To Janet Faye, my wife and best friend, who has been writing our love story for fifteen years.' Oh, Nick that's so beautiful. Thank you, darling."

His eyes were twinkling as he murmured, "Aren't you going to ask what it's about?"

"Okay," Jan obliged with a grin. "What's it about?"

He laughed, a little self-consciously, she thought. "It's a love story. Oh, there's enough action to keep my regular readers happy, but the romance is the heart of the story. No plots to bomb the UN, no terrorists passing themselves off as meter readers—just two people finding each other, beating the odds and coming out winners."

"Like us?" Jan could hardly speak for the tightness in her throat.

"Like us." He kissed her tenderly. "In case I

haven't mentioned it, Mrs. Alexander, I adore you. Now for surprise number two."

Taking the box from her, he replaced it with the envelope. Inside Jan found a contract.

"It's already sold? Oh, Nick, that's great! Congratulations, darling."

"Better look again," he advised soberly. "I haven't received the contract for *my* book yet."

Frowning in confusion, Jan began to skim over the first page of the contract. When she reached the second line, her mouth opened with a gasp. "What...?"

"While you were gone, I gathered up a bunch of your photos. Allen helped pick which ones to send to my agent. He called the day he got them, said they were dynamite and he didn't think he'd have any trouble getting a publisher interested. Obviously he was right. The contract came two days ago. Looks like we'll have to add a room to the house," he teased. "I'd thought we could turn the spare room into an office for you, but now that we'll need it for a nursery...."

Jan threw her arms around his neck, the contract still in her hand. "Oh, you wonderful, wonderful man! What did I ever do to deserve you!" She kissed him soundly, then sat back. "You know, we could both move our 'offices' to the bungalow. That way, we'd have two extra rooms in the house. We may need them someday."

"Now that's a provocative statement if I've ever heard one. Planning to fill the house with kids, are you?" He didn't sound at all disturbed by the idea.

"Why not? We could have Dawg III, and then Dawg IV...who knows, we may even get around to *Nick*, Jr., eventually."

A deep laugh rumbled up from Nick's chest. He kissed the end of her nose, rocking her gently from side to side. "I'd never have believed I could be this happy," he murmured huskily. "I swear, woman, if you ever leave me again I'll be after you like a shot, and when I get you home I really will use chains to keep you where you belong."

Jan snuggled against his chest, hugging him tight. "The chains are already there, around my heart," she told him softly. "And the funny thing is, I don't mind them at all. They make me feel very secure, wanted and needed."

"And loved, I hope," Nick whispered.

"And loved." She pressed her lips to his chest, then contentedly rested her head in the curve of his shoulder.

And then there were no more words, or the need for any. Between them, a baby who for the rest of his life would bear the unlikely nickname of Dawg, Jr.—D. J. for short—kicked out in protest at the way he was being jostled about—or maybe it was in celebration.

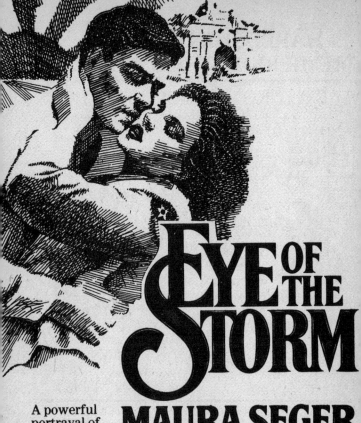

EYE OF THE STORM

MAURA SEGER

A powerful
portrayal of
the events of
World War II in the
Pacific, *Eye of the Storm* is a riveting story of how love
triumphs over hatred. In this, the first of a three book
chronicle, Army nurse Maggie Lawrence meets Marine
Sgt. Anthony Gargano. Despite military regulations
against fraternization, they resolve to face together
whatever lies ahead.... Also known by her fans as
Laurel Winslow, Sara Jennings, Anne MacNeil and
Jenny Bates, Maura Seger, author of this searing novel,
was named by ROMANTIC TIMES as 1984's Most
Versatile Romance Author.

At your favorite bookstore in March.

EYE-B-1